Also by Malcolm Rose

HURRICANE FORCE

MALCOLM ROSE
THE DEATH GENE

SIMON AND SCHUSTER

SIMON AND SCHUSTER

First published in Great Britain by Simon & Schuster UK Ltd, 2006
A CBS COMPANY

1 3 5 7 9 10 8 6 4 2

Simon & Schuster UK Ltd
Africa House
64-78 Kingsway
London WC2B 6AH

A CIP catalogue record for this book is available from the British Library

ISBN 0-689-87509-6
EAN 9780689875090

Typeset in Palatino by M Rules
Printed and bound in Great Britain by
Cox & Wyman Ltd, Reading, Berks

For Bob Johnstone

AUTHOR'S NOTE

Around the world, several research groups are trying to do what no human has yet done: to create a new living being from non-living substances. They are aiming to make a simple set of artificial chromosomes and put it into the dead shell of a once living organism to create a totally new and synthetic life form. If successful, such audacious experiments will illuminate what life really is, how it began and what it means to be alive. The race to make a new species from scratch will be watched keenly by many different groups. These include people with questions about the secrets of life, religious believers who are uncomfortable with scientists taking the role of creators, entrepreneurs who would like to develop synthetic organisms into slaves for cleaning up the environment or treating ill health, and those who fear designer life forms might escape from the laboratory and cause havoc in the community. However, some of the most enthusiastic onlookers may well be terrorists and military groups who could use the new technology to tailor-make a living weapon for germ warfare.

Several real institutions are mentioned in these pages but the events and characters associated with them are entirely fictional.

PART 1
GENESIS

CHAPTER 1

The deafening sounds of revving engines and crashing cars had bombarded Karl Stephenson and Finn Pallister all morning. Their supercharged motors had spun alarmingly off the road into fields, rolled over spectacularly, and smashed noisily into each other, trees, bridges and spectators. Racing mud-splattered souped-up rally cars, the boys had yelled and cheered, fists clenched, arms raised in the air, making almost as much din as the surround-sound system on Karl's PlayStation.

But the computer-generated racket from the loud-speakers was nothing compared to a real collision. The game's artificial sound was designed to get their hearts pounding, to make them yearn for more. The hideous sound of a genuine impact in the road that Saturday lunchtime, right in front of them, would stop their hearts, make them wish they were somewhere else.

Karl and Finn were on their way to the city centre to buy a few things before the match. They didn't get the opportunity, though. Walking down Brownlow Hill, they were waylaid by the accident and its aftermath.

It wasn't exciting like the sights and sounds of the rally game. It was horrible and ugly. A woman, breathless from running, made a frantic careless dash across the main road, right in front of an oncoming car. The driver hit his brakes and his tyres let out an ear-splitting squeal, grotesquely high-pitched. Blue smoke spewed from under the wheels and the air filled with the appalling stench of burning rubber. That was something else that shocked the boys. PlayStations don't come equipped with the revolting smell of road accidents.

The motorist didn't stand a chance of stopping in time, or of avoiding the woman. The noise of his bumper slamming into her legs was truly nauseating. Scooped up by the car, she pivoted above the bonnet. Her head came down and smacked into the windscreen, leaving a crimson stain. Then, feet first, she rolled right over the top of the car and landed like a heavy sack in the road behind. The driver began to pitch forward as soon as his wheels locked but the exploding air bag knocked him back into his seat. Out cold with shock, his head lolled to one side.

The two fifteen-year-olds stopped, open-mouthed, stunned beyond words. All colour drained from their faces. The injured woman lay just a couple of metres away from them and her open eyes stared at them, begging them to go to her. Completely at a loss, they swallowed nervously and then stepped gingerly into the silenced road and squatted beside her. It was a dreadful sight. This time, the blood was authentic, dark red and syrupy, a life leaking away. This time, the victim wouldn't regenerate when the game began again. She was a real woman with real skin, flesh and bone and, somewhere, a real family and friends. Hers was a fragile life that didn't stand a chance against the momentum of a tonne of metal careering downhill. She was dying.

Finn and Karl didn't know precisely what told them that her wounds were fatal. Yes, there was blood spreading from her head. Yes, there was a leg at a crazy angle. But her worst injuries were internal, unseen. It was probably the desperation in her eyes that told them she was beyond help.

Even though she was dying, she strained her neck and lifted her head from the filthy surface of the road, out of the sickening red pool. One of her blackened cheeks had caved in entirely. If she felt pain, she ignored it as she looked around in panic. Karl and Finn gulped and followed the line of her eyes, past the developing traffic jam. Three men were rushing towards her. The boys didn't know who they were, what type of men they were, but they weren't paramedics for sure. The woman pulled a notebook – about the size of an exercise book but far thicker – from inside her coat and held it out towards the boys with a shaking hand.

Puzzled, Karl and Finn gazed at the book and then at each other.

In a ghastly, gurgling voice, she whispered, 'Take it! Don't let them get it.' Her fading eyes glanced towards the onrushing men.

With hollow stomachs, still Finn and Karl hesitated.

'Go on!' As a final gesture, she thrust it at them again.

Deciding that there was a way to help her after all, Karl reached forward and, out of sympathy, grasped the heavy notebook as if he were reluctantly accepting a gift. He shuddered because it felt like grave robbing.

There was relief in the woman's drained face but she wasn't at peace. She would die without closure, without contentment. 'Go. Hurry!'

The three men were bearing down on them. One shouted at the top of his voice, 'Hey! Leave her alone. Don't touch . . .'

A driver at the back of the stationary queue sounded his horn, long and impatient.

Karl and Finn didn't wait. With a momentary glance at each other, they agreed silently to leg it. When they got to their feet and spun around, they gasped. A small crowd of people had gathered behind them. One woman was talking rapidly and animatedly into her mobile phone, calling for an ambulance. The others looked dazed and horrified. And they stared accusingly at Finn and Karl as if they were responsible for the crash. When the two boys shouldered their way through the statues, someone shouted venomously at them, 'You can't leave. You're witnesses.'

Glimpsing the three men bearing down on them, they ignored the remark. After all, they were carrying out the dying woman's wish. Finn led the charge down the road towards Liverpool's shopping centre.

Their heartbeats accelerated again. One of the men had stopped beside the victim, kneeling down to examine her in front of the nosy bystanders. The other two were giving chase. There was nothing enjoyable, no fun at all, in *this* race. Karl and Finn didn't know what they were running from and they didn't know what would happen if the men actually caught up with them. The boys suspected that they could not risk finding out.

'This way!' Finn cried. Not waiting for the little red man to turn green – and not considering what had just happened to the woman in Brownlow Hill – he dashed across Renshaw Street, cutting through the endless stream of cars, buses and taxis.

Horns sounded and Karl gulped. He was fearful of the traffic but even more fearful of the men thirty metres behind him. With the notebook in his fist, he followed his friend, hoping he wouldn't meet the same fate as the woman who'd shoved it at him.

They headed towards Central Station, pushing their way through the crowds of shoppers outside John Lewis's. It was late February and everyone had wrapped themselves up in thick coats against the cold day.

Car horns blared again as, further back, the two men also charged across the busy street.

Usually, Finn and Karl knew the kind of people they were trying to outrun: the police, older boys, gangs. Not this time. The men were an unknown quantity. At the Merseyrail station, Finn glanced around. Noticing the pedestrian lights turning green, he saw his chance. 'The shopping arcade. We'll lose them in there.'

They sprinted across the road, swerved round the fruit stall, and darted into Clayton Square Shopping Centre. There, the boys thrust their way through the shoppers, past the booths selling handbags and trinkets in the middle of the aisle. Overhead, someone was bashing out sloppy ragtime piano in the first-floor café. In the distance, they could make out a siren.

Checking over his shoulder, Karl said, 'Can't see them. It's working!'

Not looking where he was going, Karl crashed into an old man by the escalator and the dead woman's notebook spilled from his hand. It went flying through the open doorway of Virgin Records. 'Bugger!' Karl muttered to himself. Then, apologising to the startled man, he dashed after it.

Finn stopped running and cried, 'What are you . . .?' When he realised what had happened, he turned round, keeping a lookout. With a sinking feeling, he saw the mystery men entering the arcade. They looked rough and mean and impatient, like gangsters.

Inside the record shop, a girl was bending down to pick up the notebook but Karl shouted, 'It's okay. It's mine.' She was nice-looking, though, so he gave her a big grin before he grabbed it and straightened up.

At his side, Finn said, 'They're coming! I saw them.'

'Did they see *you*?'

'I think so. Come on. Out the back way.'

They raced out of the shop, scattering pigeons from the traffic-free road. Opposite was the rear entrance to St John's Precinct.

'I know,' Finn panted. 'In here.'

By the time that the boys flew into the mall, the gangsters had emerged from Clayton Square and got a fix on them.

Karl was the clever one of the pair, but Finn had always had a knack for getting out of trouble. As Finn aimed for the market's circle of snack bars, Karl followed without question. In the centre of the precinct, there were seats, fountains and mirrors. Lots of mirrors, all at peculiar angles, making the place look much larger and more confusing than it really was. Like a fairground maze.

CHAPTER 2

By the fountain, Finn and Karl huddled in an inconspicuous niche behind two sets of mirrors. They believed that they could be seen only from one narrow angle. They also believed that, if the men threatened to spot them, they could creep along to the next table to keep out of their field of view. Trying to control their gasping, they waited like cornered but concealed prey.

Further down the walkway, the chasing men had slowed to walking pace, wandering through the market, peering briefly into every shop. One checked out the stores on the left, the other took care of the ones on the right. Occasionally, they glanced across at each other and shook their heads. They looked determined, not the type to admit defeat.

The wait seemed endless. Shaking with nerves, Karl watched the comings and goings at the other tables but he couldn't get the image of the woman's blackened and sunken cheek out of his mind. 'Have they gone?' he asked. 'Maybe they've given up.'

'We can't risk it. Not yet,' Finn replied.

A few minutes later, three attractive girls stripped off their coats, revealing Everton shirts, and settled at a neighbouring table with Cokes. Normally, Karl would have elbowed Finn and nodded towards them, but now he didn't feel in the mood.

Neither Karl nor Finn had anticipated that the men would split up and go opposite ways round the ring of shops and cafés. When the first one appeared at the point where he could spin round and see the boys, they inched back towards the girls, directly into the view of the second man.

There was a loud shout of, 'There they are!'

The boys clattered across the seating area, flinging chairs and stools aside. They sprinted down the other arm of St John's Precinct with their stalkers barely twenty metres behind.

They raced past Woolworths, up the steps and shot back across Renshaw Street where it transformed into Lime Street. If they went to the right, they'd be perilously close to the site of the accident where they'd be caught by police, recognised by the crowd or collared by the third man who might still be lurking nearby. Instinct made them go left, heading for the mainline railway station.

They barged in through the large glass doors, against the flow of arriving Aston Villa supporters. Karl's eyes darted up to the clock and television screen. A train bound for Manchester, Sheffield and Norwich would be leaving in one minute from the nearest platform. It gave him an idea. 'Come on!' Karl cried at Finn.

They dashed round the corner towards Platform 9 but, before they were out of sight, Karl made sure that the two men had seen them.

Rushing for the train, Finn gasped, 'This is crazy. Are you sure?'

Karl was smiling now. 'Trust me.'

He slammed his palm against the *open* button and the door slid back with a hiss. The boys jumped into the rear coach, but Karl poked his head out of the door to check that the men had seen them boarding the train. When they both pointed at him and accelerated, Karl ducked back inside. He turned to face Finn's accusing expression.

'Now we're trapped,' Finn muttered. 'They've got us.'

Karl brushed past him, saying, 'Hurry up.'

Karl led the charge down the aisle, turning the heads of scowling passengers. An intercom voice was listing all of the places where the train would stop, starting with Warrington. By the time they tore into the front coach, the voice announced, 'This train is about to depart.'

The two men had also got on board. They were smirking and making their way unhurriedly and deliberately through the first coach.

The boys belted half of the length of the front coach

and Karl flung himself against the door button again. Behind him, Finn finally understood Karl's plan. Almost as soon as they'd leapt down onto the platform, the door slid shut and the train began to move, painfully slowly at first, out of the station.

The two men were caught inside, banging on the door release in frustration.

Breathless, Karl and Finn waved them goodbye.

The boys' self-congratulatory smiles faded slowly as they remembered how the chase had begun.

To avoid Brownlow Hill on the way home, Finn and Karl cut up beside the station and returned to the flats by Copperas Hill. Karl's fourth-floor apartment looked over the concrete lump that was the Brontë Youth and Community Centre and towards the spiky crown of the Roman Catholic cathedral. Sitting on Karl's unmade bed in his incredibly messy room, the lads flicked through the pages of the bloodstained notebook and Finn muttered impatiently, 'What is this?'

It was handwritten and seemed to be an incomprehensible record of some scientific experiments. If it belonged to the dead woman, if she'd written it, her name was Eve Perry, according to the inside front cover. Dr Eve A Perry, School of Biological Sciences, the University of Liverpool. Underneath a faint number was written in pencil: 1132.

Finn's finger followed the top two lines of text as he

read aloud the heading on the first page, stumbling over some of the words, 'Stage 1. Procedure for removing the entire genome from the bacterium, *Mycoplasma genitalium.*'

'Wow. Going to need a dictionary,' Karl replied.

Finn shrugged and lost interest. 'I don't know why we risked our necks for a science lesson. It might as well be Chinese. Rubbish. I can't be bothered.'

'You've got to be joking. She died to give us this. And muggers chased us halfway across the city for it. She probably copped it because she was running away from them as well. It's got to be hot stuff.' Karl glanced at some pages towards the end of the laboratory notebook. 'Don't know why, though,' he admitted.

'Look,' Finn said, stabbing the page with his forefinger. 'Big words. What's genome and mycoplasma? And genitalium. Isn't that rude?'

Karl sat up straight. 'Hope so. Makes it worth having a go.'

Finn sniffed and thought about it for a few seconds. 'You could show it to Mr Dee at school. He knows posh words.'

Karl shook his head. 'We can't show it to anyone. Not till we know what it's about. Could be dangerous.'

'How do you mean?'

'If people know we've got it, we might end up like . . .' He read the scientist's name from the inside front cover again. 'Eve Perry.'

'Those blokes already know we've got it,' said Finn. 'And they looked pretty pissed off.'

'But they don't know us.'

'I bet they're out looking. Or they will be when they get back from Warrington. Even more pissed off.'

'What do you want to do, then?' Karl asked.

'Chuck it. Forget the whole thing.'

'They'll still come looking for us.'

Finn replied, 'Yeah but, if they find us, we won't have it.'

Karl sighed. 'Bet that won't save us. Nah. *You* forget it if you like. I'm going to keep it.'

Finn shrugged again. 'Up to you.'

'Just don't tell anyone about it. It's between you and me. No one else.'

'Sure,' said Finn, eyeing Karl's PlayStation again. It was an old model, nicked from a market stall, but Finn didn't have anything like it. 'Fancy another game? We've got time before the match.'

Karl frowned. 'Don't really feel like it any more.'

CHAPTER 3

In the darkened room, Bennett muttered, 'Scientists *always* make a copy of their lab notebooks. In case the original gets lost, goes up in flames or something. Always. Sometimes, they keep the original at work and the duplicate at home. That way, if one place gets burned to the ground, the other copy's safe.'

The three men had failed to get the original notebook from the two interfering lads so, for the moment, they were searching for the duplicate. They'd broken into Dr Perry's house and they would risk spending most of the night there, going through every desk, file, shelf, drawer and cupboard in silence by torchlight until they found what they wanted. If necessary, they'd search under carpets, floorboards, mattresses and cushions, in the loft and garage, in every conceivable hiding place. They would have dismantled the entire house if they could have done it without being discovered. That's how important a second copy of the laboratory notebook was.

Finding themselves empty-handed after the car accident, Kerven, Smith and Bennett had gone back to

Perry's laboratory at the university on Saturday night and searched every centimetre. They'd found plenty of notebooks but not a duplicate of the important one, so tonight they were trying Plan B: turning her home upside down.

One of the rooms in Eve Perry's rural bungalow in West Kirby was a study. While Kerven searched the rest of the house, Bennett and Smith concentrated their efforts on this one room. They had already set her computer to search for files containing the text, *new life form*, but it hadn't turned up anything significant. A search for files containing the word *Mycoplasma* was finding vast numbers of documents and, later, Bennett would open each one but he wasn't hopeful because he expected the information he needed would be hand-written.

By three-thirty in the morning, Bennett was frustrated as usual. In the third drawer of Eve's enormous filing cabinet he'd found only letters about research publications. There was desperation in his tone as he whispered to himself, 'Where *is* the damn thing?'

Smith was sitting in a halo of light, methodically combing the drawers of her desk. With ruffled hair and dirty clothing, he looked anything but a saint. 'Well, if we don't find it here tonight, she either destroyed it or hid it pretty good.'

Bennett glanced at him gravely but did not reply. Not yet willing to admit defeat, he slid open the bottom drawer on its metal runner. With strong latex gloves stretched tight over both hands, he angled the torch-light down onto the hanging files. Lots of them. He winced at the sight of so many papers to examine but he removed the first file and began to read it carefully.

At a quarter past five they declared the place clean. The second copy of Dr Perry's laboratory notebook had eluded them. It wasn't in the house and she hadn't transferred the information to her computer. Now, they had to sneak away before dawn, before the Wirral woke and discovered them.

After last night's antics, Angus Kerven had a plaster on his torn forefinger. 'It's back to finding the original copy, then,' he said softly, suppressing a cough as they headed for the door with the busted lock.

'Yes,' Smith replied. 'It looks like those lads have got the only copy.'

'But how to find them?' Bennett whispered. 'We can hardly go to the cop shop and ask if they've traced them yet.'

'We'll sort that later,' Smith said in a hushed voice. Cautiously, he put his head around the back door and then told the other two, 'All clear. We're out of here.'

CHAPTER 4

Brilliant controversial scientist dies

Eve A Perry

The goal of understanding the nature of life suffered a considerable set-back on Saturday when Dr Eve Perry, controversial biologist in the School of Biological Sciences, died tragically at the age of twenty-nine. She was involved in a traffic accident near her laboratory at the University of Liverpool.

Although very young for an academic scientist, Dr Perry had already gained a formidable reputation in the field of genetics. As a talented research student at the University of Cambridge, she helped to decode the human genome – the chemical recipe for making human characteristics. After taking up the post of lecturer in genetics at Liverpool, she initiated her own research programme and sequenced the genes of several simple organisms, such as *Mycoplasma* bacteria and the malaria parasite, providing new lines of research for curing malaria.

Dr Perry worked alone so her most recent research will remain incomplete. She declared at an international genetics conference last year that her purpose was to create life from scratch. Dr Perry could consider such an ambitious target because her work on primitive organisms had allowed her to identify the minimum gene set necessary to define a reproducing life form. She had indicated at the conference that her aim was to make those genes artificially and produce from them a new species that would benefit the world. She hinted that she could design bacteria that would feed on pollution and hence destroy it, or consume carbon dioxide to reduce global warming. She also stated her plan to make an organism with genes that would produce hydrogen, solving the world's clean energy needs. Although creating a new species raises deep scientific and ethical issues, an ethics panel concluded in 1999 that it was not wrong to construct life for such beneficial humanitarian reasons.

Dr Perry's work was considered controversial because any new synthetic organism could pose dangers for existing life forms, including human beings. Dr Perry's intentions were unquestionably humanitarian but there was a concern that her project could be hijacked for bioterrorism. In the wrong hands, her techniques could have been used by terrorists to design a virulent and deadly life form. Dr Perry acknowledged this possibility and vowed never to disclose all the details of her work, so that it could not be subverted for military purposes.

As a result, we may never be sure if she succeeded in making a synthetic being. Because of her untimely death, any secrets of life that she may have revealed will have to wait until an equally gifted biologist succeeds her. Regrettably, her imaginative environmental solutions will also be postponed.

Wedded to her subject, Dr Perry did not leave children but she is survived by her parents.

In the same newspaper, there was an appeal for two teenage boys at the scene of the accident to come forward. Eyewitnesses described them as white, fourteen to seventeen years old, with average height and build. One had very short light-coloured hair and a boisterous appearance. He was thought to be wearing jeans and a blue sweatshirt. The other was dressed in sports gear and had longer, untidy dark hair. Both were reported to have run down Brownlow Hill towards the shopping area, apparently pursued by two or three men. The newspaper article made it clear that the police would also like to interview those men.

'Untidy!' Karl exclaimed, running his hand through his curly hair. 'Huh. Someone had better get their eyesight tested. And where does it say irresistible to girls?'

'You'd better get it cut. And dyed blond.'

'And you ought to grow yours right now. Or get a wig. Anyway, I'm taller than you,' Karl added, still complaining that his description in the newspaper wasn't sufficiently flattering. 'I'm above average.'

Ignoring his mate, Finn pointed at the picture with the caption, 'Dr Eve Perry – tragically killed in a road accident.'

'Yep,' said Karl. 'That's her all right.' He scanned down the obituary, then added, 'It says here she was going to make some sort of new life.'

'What? Like Frankenstein? I saw the film on telly.'

Karl was concentrating on the newspaper article. 'There's something about *Mycoplasma*. That's what's in her notebook. It's a bacterium or something. Listen! "In the wrong hands, her techniques could have been used by terrorists to design a virulent and deadly life form." That pretty much tells us who those blokes were.'

'Does it?' Finn asked.

'Bet that's who chased us,' Karl replied. 'Terrorists.

We stopped them getting their hands on her secret plans. Reckon we saved the country.'

'Yeah. But we're still wanted, like criminals.'

It didn't cross their minds to hand the book in to the police, or to volunteer themselves for questioning. They didn't trust the law. They were always being stopped and quizzed or moved on by cops – even when they were doing nothing wrong. It was because they came from the wrong side of town, wore the wrong clothes, and hung out in the wrong places. And they'd both been cautioned in the past for shoplifting. That gave the police a licence to hassle them at every opportunity.

Anyway, Karl wanted to make sense of the notes and Finn didn't fancy being blamed for nicking them. And both of them guessed that the terrorists would be keeping a watch on the police station in case they turned up.

Karl reminded him, 'We promised to keep our traps shut. Remember? It's just between you and me. Let's keep it that way.'

Finn shrugged, then glanced at his watch. 'It's time.'

'Suppose so.' Karl stood up. He wasn't sure if he was still eager to spend two hours every Monday evening at the Brontë Youth and Community Centre. At first, the Teen and Toddler Scheme – meant to discourage teenage pregnancies – had seemed like a great idea. It was a sure-fire way of meeting girls. Yet the sessions had turned out to be more like hard work than a dating opportunity.

Once a week, every boy had to 'adopt' a toddler and look after him for a couple of hours in the Youth Centre. The girls got to look after the female babies. Clearly, the idea was to put teenagers off parenthood by proving that children are incredibly demanding. It was also about kindling community spirit and accepting responsibility for another being.

The trouble was, Karl and Finn weren't convinced that the toddlers were human at all. The little aliens issued piercing sounds, crying for food, drink, their parents, sleep, a teething ring, or a toy that another small creature was hogging. They insisted on grasping and tasting everything that had been put out of their reach. They drenched and dirtied their nappies without warning yet with great glee. Once they'd finished screaming for their mums and warmed to their teenage minders, they demanded attention all of the time. And, because a devious intelligence was developing in their heads, they worked out that they could get away with all sorts of bad behaviour. Mostly, they wanted to do precisely what they'd been told not to do. They were obstinate, obsessive, outlandish and, despite it all, cute. In a way.

But the scheme to prevent unwanted children left hardly any time for Karl to chat up a girl called Shaughney Willett with short blonde hair and big round earrings. The hoops were silvery red, twice the size of the human ear and they caught on her shoulders whenever she turned her head. Right now, she was holding up her particular bundle of fun, sniffing its rear end and grimacing.

Karl was having an easier time of it. He'd got Adam – every lad's favourite. Adam Satchwell had taken to the scheme straightaway. No screaming for mum, no tantrums. Just a tiny offered hand and a face-filling grin for any boy who'd play endlessly with the foam football. The only chore was picking him up every time he kicked the ball and fell over. That was most of the time. His worst behaviour was a nasty fit of coughing. Even though a miniature monster was not plaguing Karl, it was hard to chat up a girl when she had her nose crinkled up against a lively nappy.

Karl whispered to Adam, 'If I were you, pal, I wouldn't bother to grow up. You've got to go to school, organise your own toileting, and try to get to grips with girls. Nightmare.'

Afterwards, with all the little devils back in proper custody, Karl decided to try his luck. He changed his mind, though, when he heard Shaughney chatting to a friend called Grace.

'I'll tell you what's wrong with boys,' Shaughney was muttering vehemently. 'What do they say to a boy who has lots of sex? Respect! What do they call a girl who has lots of sex? Slag! Even a boy's puny brain should see that's offside. But they don't.'

Karl hesitated, turned, and went back towards Finn.

'What's up?' Finn asked.

Karl shrugged. 'In a mood. Not a good time.'

The two girls glanced at them across the room. Grace smiled tentatively but Shaughney frowned as if she were suspicious of them.

'You bottled it!' Finn exclaimed.

'Nah,' Karl said defensively. 'Think the dirty nappy went to her head.'

Behind the boys, Adam coughed and spluttered in his pushchair, sharing his germs generously with the neighbourhood.

Karl put up his hand, almost waved at the child, and said, 'See you.' Then he felt foolish.

Finn sniggered at his mate. 'You're going soft.'

'Let's go. I want to have another look at that notebook. Compare it with the bit in the newspaper. See if I can make sense of it.'

Finn groaned. 'Don't blame me if your head explodes.'

'Are you coming?'

With heavy sarcasm, he replied, 'What a tragedy. I can't. I've got to walk the dog and visit Nan.'

'Yeah. Your Bouncer needs a nappy as well.'

Finn grinned widely as he said, 'So does Nan.'

CHAPTER 5

The front of the block where Karl and Finn lived was straight up and down, and the roof was flat. The whole uninspiring building was one large perfect cube with five rows of windows spaced at exact intervals. Every window was divided horizontally into four panes by identical white frames. Some of the glass in the rectangles was cracked. From a distance, the place looked like a prison with white bars for every cell. Outside, there were seven To Let signs. Three had been pulled to absurd angles. Another had been uprooted altogether.

The hollow bass of a rap song boomed down from the flat above Karl's head. Whenever Karl put his hand lightly on a wall, or the ceiling of his room by standing on his bed, he could feel the vibration as well as hear it. The white guy who lived upstairs worked in a fish-and-chip shop and thought he was incredibly hip. His music, mannerisms and speech were all borrowed from a different culture. To Karl, he seemed more sad than cool.

Karl snipped Eve Perry's obituary out of the newspaper and laid the flimsy cutting on the floor alongside her weighty notebook. Then he got down onto the shabby carpet, chin resting on both fists, to compare the two articles. His eyes flitted from one to the other, from the difficult-to-understand piece in the paper to the impossible-to-understand experimental details in the laboratory book.

As far as he could make out, the biologist had started with a bug called *Mycoplasma genitalium* and scooped out all of its genes. That was like sucking the innards out of a person, giving her a dead empty shell to stuff with new life. But Eve Perry was nothing like Frankenstein. She was messing around with a tiny germ, not assembling a human being. Then there were incomprehensible sections about base pairs, short DNA strands, sequencers and synthesis. He sank rapidly into a quagmire of technical information.

He flicked through some of the later sections. Near the middle of the notebook, he focused on another heading. 'Stage 2. Injection of synthetic genome into emptied *Mycoplasma genitalium*: creation of *Mycoplasma perrium*.' So, she did produce a new life – and named it after herself. Karl thought of her as a single mum, giving the newborn her surname but converting *Perry* into *perrium* to make it sound more scientific. Further on, she'd written, 'Stage 3. Testing of *Mycoplasma perrium* for ability to survive and reproduce.' That couldn't be the end of the story, though, because there were still pages and pages of densely scribbled notes.

Karl stood up and stretched. He'd had enough.

There was an eight-second lull in the bass throb from upstairs before it began again.

March arrived in a sudden squall. The wind and rain seemed to come at Finn and Karl from all angles. The walk to school on Tuesday was more like a battle. Finn was all for giving up, getting a bus and bunking off for the day in the city centre but Karl kept him going. He wanted to do a web search in the school library.

But when he entered *Mycoplasma*, he got lots of sites about pneumonia. It didn't take a genius to work it out. A bug that shared a first name with Eve Perry's bacterium, *Mycoplasma pneumoniae*, hung about in the human respiratory tract and caused the illness. Karl wasn't interested in pneumonia, so he tried a different search. This time, he used the full name – *Mycoplasma genitalium* – and the search threw up tens of thousands of hits. The top fits seemed to be about genetics. Yet, when he clicked on any of them to find out more, the computer refused to send him to the site. Instead, the school's software told him that the contents of the website were inappropriate.

Making Karl and Finn jump, Mr Dee looked over their shoulders and said, 'Mmm. Bacteria. Nice. All God's creatures great and small . . .'

For a moment, Karl considered trying to hide the results of his search. But it was too late. Mr Dee had already got a good look. Karl had agreed with Finn not to show Dr Perry's notebook to the science teacher and to keep quiet about the whole business. Yet Karl needed help to understand what was going on. He glanced at his friend and then decided to grill Mr Dee without giving anything away. 'We're after *Mycoplasma genitalium* but the filter's kicked in. It's stopping us seeing anything.'

'Yeah,' Finn chipped in because he thought that he ought to say something.

Mr Dee gazed at them for a moment and then seemed to make up his mind that they weren't mucking about. He smiled. 'The school doesn't want you delving into anything genital. Quite right. But if you were up to something improper, I suspect there'd be a hundred slang words you'd enter before you thought of genitals.'

Finn wasn't sure what the teacher meant. He took his door key out of his pocket and fiddled with it instead.

Trying not to snigger or redden with embarrassment or guilt, Karl asked, 'What is it, *Mycoplasma genitalium*?'

'That's not a question I hear every day – and I'm mighty surprised it's you two taking an interest – but I'm fairly sure it's a single-cell organism that lives in people's genital tracts. It's natural and harmless, I think. Why do you want to know?'

Karl hesitated for an instant. 'Oh, just saw about it in the paper.'

'Ah. That'll be Eve Perry's obituary.'

Karl nodded.

'I saw it as well. You weren't . . .' Looking thoughtful, the teacher paused.

'What?' But Karl knew what was coming. He could see it in Mr Dee's face. He was thinking about the newspaper report. Two white teenage boys, fourteen to seventeen years old, average height and build; one with short fair hair in jeans and a sweatshirt; the other with long dark hair and wearing sports gear.

'Were you involved in her accident? Were you there? Is that why you're interested?'

Karl laughed. 'It was Saturday, sir!'

'Yes?'

'Everton versus Aston Villa. We were getting ready for the match.' Karl shook his head. 'No, it was just that my mum pointed out the bit in the paper. Struck me as weird. You know, making a new life form and all that.'

'Yeah,' Finn agreed.

Mr Dee seemed satisfied. 'Well, yes, weird's one word for it. Science throws up all sorts of ethical issues these days.' He gazed at Finn for a moment and then said, 'Put your key away before you lose it.'

Finn shrugged and slipped it back into his pocket.

Still curious, Karl asked, 'Did you know her, sir?'

'No.'

'What's a minimum gene set?'

30

'The smallest number of genes that'll make a living creature, like the smallest motor that'll run a car. Some biologists think you could make a simple bug in a lab.' He shrugged. 'Perhaps Dr Perry did. Very dangerous ground.'

As far as teachers went, Mr Dee wasn't too bad. He was strict and he grumbled a lot about kids' attitudes, but he drove a wicked Ferrari. Okay, it wasn't new and it had seen better days, but it still made up for all his negatives. So, Karl carried on. 'What would happen if she did?'

Mr Dee perched on the edge of the seat next to Karl and Finn. 'Look at it this way. If you rip all the pages out of a book and stick totally different pages between the covers, it'd look the same but you'd have another story altogether. A new species.'

Karl thought for a moment. 'Like rebooting a computer with a new operating system?'

Mr Dee smiled again. 'Yes. Good analogy.'

Rain battered the window behind the monitor as if nature were trying to get at them.

'The question is, why bother?' said Karl.

The teacher raised both arms in an exaggerated shrug. 'I suppose, scientific curiosity over the nature of life rates pretty near the top of the list. But, you know, some say you should leave this sort of thing to God. Some say science should only be used in the service of God, not against Him. According to Dr Perry's obituary, she wanted to engineer an organism that would benefit the world. Think of a tiny thing that'll lunch on pollution, breaking it down. Or make clean hydrogen fuel. That would be a valuable little bug.'

Finn leapt into the conversation. 'My nan got that superbug thing. The one that you catch in hospital. She died last night,' he stated bluntly.

Mr Dee's face went into deep-concern mode. 'I'm sorry to hear that, Finn. Your grandmother . . .'

'Great grandma,' Finn said, correcting him.

The teacher spoke softly, apparently not sure how to react. 'Bacteria can be very destructive, I'm afraid, and hard to get rid of. I suspect your great grandma got MRSA . . .'

'Yeah. That's it.'

'It's an infection that doesn't respond to antibiotics, I'm afraid. But bacteria aren't all like MRSA. Having said that, the nasty ones sometimes pass their DNA on to the harmless ones, teaching them bad habits. If you think about your computer analogy, Karl, they exchange programs so they can get new instructions.'

'I've been thinking,' Karl replied. 'How do you prove something's alive?'

At once, Finn answered, 'You stab it in the bum and see if it moves.'

'If you were unconscious, Finn, you'd fail that test,' Mr Dee replied. 'No. An organism's alive if it can make copies of itself, get energy from nutrients, and evolve –

that means, adapt to changes. They'd be the main tests: reproduction, metabolism and self-improvement. Most living creatures grow and react to heat, light or sound as well. You could imagine all sorts of checks, even if the thing doesn't have a backside and you don't have a handy needle.' Suddenly he looked at his watch and stood up. 'I've got to go, boys. If you want to learn more about all this, I can point you in the right direction, if you've decided to scale uncharted academic heights all of a sudden. Come and see me after school.'

Karl nodded. 'We'll ... think about it.' As soon as Mr Dee was out of hearing, Karl said, 'You didn't tell me about your nan.'

Finn shrugged. 'She was old.'

He didn't seem to need further explanation. A cruel and rampant germ had taken advantage of a weak and elderly woman. That was nature's way and nature didn't have a conscience.

Some of Eve Perry's notes made more sense to Karl now. Dr Perry knew her homemade bacteria were alive and kicking because she'd put them in a nutrient soup, watched them multiply and completed some DNA tests on the offspring. At the end of the part proving their ability to survive and reproduce, she had written, 'Safety Issues. (1) Development of a drug for the death gene – see Notebook 7A. (2) Checking *Mycoplasma perrium* does not possess a gene enabling it to attach to human cells.' Even if the jargon prevented Karl from understanding the section, he was pleased that safety was on her mind. He gathered from the write-up that her new life form couldn't stick to people's insides so it couldn't infect anyone and he thought she'd made a chemical that would kill it off.

It sounded clever and controlled. But Finn's nan had been infected by a bacterium and clever medicine hadn't made a difference. Despite all of the hospital's powerful antibiotic drugs, the bug kept nibbling away at her until she died. On top of that, why were terrorists keen to get their hands on the instruction book if *Mycoplasma perrium* was harmless? The newspaper called them bioterrorists and Karl was sure that's what the three mystery men must be.

Karl got up to draw his curtains. Before he shut out the concrete and tarmac terrain, he peered carefully up and down the street. There were three women in identical, very short skirts shivering under the streetlamp at the kerbside and a group of revellers smoking and drinking, probably on their way to a party. The shady guy loitering on the corner of Brontë Street dealt in different sorts of drugs altogether. He was there most nights. Nothing unusual. Karl snapped the curtains shut as if he could keep the sleazy adult world at bay.

CHAPTER 6

Weston Smith and Curtis Bennett took it in turns to linger outside the police station in case two lads showed up with a fat blue notebook. Angus Kerven was trying a different tactic to locate the boys and the laboratory information. Smith had told him to cruise up and down Brownlow Hill, occasionally driving slowly through the neighbouring estates, to check out gangs of boys hanging around the place. Kerven thought that he was wasting his time. He thought he'd get arrested for kerb-crawling before he caught sight of the two lads. But he was wrong.

He turned left just before the Metropolitan Cathedral and the Royal Liverpool University Hospital. Crawling along Great Newton Street in second gear, he slammed on his brakes to get a good look at the boy coming the other way with an Alsatian at his heel. Kerven was fairly sure he was one of the teenagers who had bolted with the notebook.

He drove past the target, then turned the car round. Yet the twitchy lad had already cottoned on. He glanced over his shoulder twice at Kerven's car. That meant Kerven couldn't simply follow him home because, knowing he was being tailed, the boy would probably dash down an alley where Kerven couldn't drive. Even if he parked the car and took to his feet, the lad would escape because he'd know the entries and back streets far better than Kerven did. The youngster would soon lose him in the warren runs of the estate. Besides, Kerven didn't fancy tackling anyone with a large dog on the street where there were on-lookers and lights.

He wound down his window and accelerated briefly. Coming to a halt opposite the boy, he called out, 'Excuse me!'

The lad eyed him warily, not running away or walking towards him.

It was Bennett and Smith who had chased the boys through the city centre so, with a bit of luck, this one wouldn't recognise him.

'I just wanted to have a word about . . . Oh, sorry.' His voice was cracking up so he leaned out of the car and spat heavily onto the pavement. The big blob of saliva glistened on the slab under the streetlight.

Coming round the corner of Dansie Street, a woman pushing a buggy smiled at the boy and said, 'Hello, Finn. It *is* Finn, isn't it?'

He nodded at her.

The toddler in the pushchair put his arm out towards the dog, but his mum bent down and pulled it away, saying, 'No, Adam.' Then she glanced at Kerven suspiciously and asked Finn, 'Are you all right?'

'Fine, thanks.'

'Okay. See you.' As she walked away, she stepped on the gobbet of spit.

'Finn,' Kerven said with a smile, 'I need to talk to you and your friend about what happened on Saturday.'

And that was it.

Detecting Finn's change of mood, the Alsatian growled at Kerven in the instant before the boy took off. By the time that Kerven unbuckled his seat belt, got out of his car and locked it, Finn had shot down a dark entry. Kerven followed but when he emerged from it, he found himself in an empty street. He imagined that this Finn was an expert at dodging people who wanted to question him.

He sighed and wandered back to his car, trying to look on the bright side. He had a name and he was convinced that the boy lived somewhere in this rundown part of town.

CHAPTER 7

It was nothing like a professional production. The woman spoke straight to a cheap camera, balanced on a shelf in front of her. The film wasn't for entertainment. It was an historical and scientific record. Looking haggard and hassled, she stared straight into the camera and began her lecture.

'*Mycoplasmas* are a group of simple life forms, having a tiny set of genes. They are humble parasites living in humans and several animals, insects and plants. *Mycoplasma genitalium* is the lowest of the low. Eve Perry hollowed it out and refilled it with artificial genes that she'd made in her laboratory. The result was the first ever species made by a scientist rather than by nature. She named it *Mycoplasma perrium*.

'The synthetic bacterium should have been a celebrity like Dolly the cloned sheep but, being microscopic, it's neither photogenic nor cuddly. Yet its size belies its status as the first man-made living creature. It's an invisible and colossal achievement. And it opens up all manner of ethical issues. It started its momentous life as a harmless entity, unable to bind to animal cells. It also had a built-in death gene and highly limited functions. It was designed to feed on only one nutrient – carbon dioxide – and to use the energy to reproduce itself. That was all. Nothing else.'

She paused, thinking for a few seconds. But not for long. She looked like a woman who was anxious to get on with something else. 'There was a good idea – and a very worthy intention – behind Eve Perry's project. Given enough *Mycoplasma perrium* in the environment, it would reduce global warming by seeking out and gobbling up one of the main sources: carbon dioxide.

'The infant bacterium was confined to a laboratory in the School of Biological Sciences at the University of Liverpool. At least, it had been contained within the laboratory – and subject to a large number of tests – until three men broke in on Saturday the twenty-sixth of February. One of them, Curtis Bennett, was a disillusioned ex-scientist, but he wasn't a specialist in genetics. He was well aware of the dangers of creating an artificial life form – that was exactly why he took the action that he did – but he wasn't familiar with biological laboratory procedures. He didn't realise the dangers when one of his colleagues, thought to be Angus Kerven, broke a sealed cabinet, quite likely by accident. Kerven must have touched a dish containing *Mycoplasma perrium* within the cabinet. Perhaps he cut himself on the broken glass and placed his forefinger in his mouth to suck away a trickle of blood.

'The bacteria had no means of combining with human cells but they would have found a warm and wet temporary home between Kerven's lower lip and gum. If he had used an antibacterial mouthwash, they would have died and that would have been the end of it. But plainly he didn't. They would have tucked in behind his lip and multiplied while Kerven himself provided a generous supply of carbon dioxide simply by breathing.

'Later, stressed by the artificial microbe nesting in his mouth, Kerven spat out thousands of the tiny beings onto a pavement in Liverpool. And, by coincidence, the young mother of Adam Satchwell smeared it all over the sole of her shoe.

'Back at her flat, Caitlin Satchwell pulled off her shoes with her hands, then lifted her toddler out of his pushchair. Adam coughed violently, as he'd been doing for a week or more. Caitlin knelt down in front of her poorly child. With her finger, she wiped away the spit from his mouth and chin, not knowing that she had just spread *Mycoplasma perrium* all over his mouth and nose. She decided to take him to the Royal Liverpool University Hospital to find out why, after several visits to her GP and lots of medicine, he still had coughing fits.

'In the hospital, little Adam could have coughed the new bacteria onto the floor, where they transferred to a patient's slippers or a visitor's shoe. Maybe he coughed onto a nurse's uniform, a drinks trolley, or a piece of wheeled medical equipment. Maybe Caitlin Satchwell still had some on her hands or shoes. If so, she could have deposited it on any one of a number of seats or on a pen when she signed a treatment form.

'However it happened, *Mycoplasma perrium* came into

40

contact with a patient called Bill Garvey who had contracted the notorious MRSA superbug from Finn Pallister's great grandmother. It was then and there that Dr Eve Perry's seemingly innocuous creation met a voracious germ that had all the genetic equipment to resist antibiotics, to latch on to human cells, to infect them, and to kill. It was almost certainly within Mr Garvey that an inoffensive microbe that loved human breath swapped chemical instructions with MRSA. Its new set of genes – stolen from MRSA – turned it into a lethal organism.

'From that point, starting with Mr Garvey, Eve Perry's orphaned bacteria began to run wild.'

CHAPTER 8

To keep Adam sweet while they waited in the hospital, Caitlin treated him to a bottle of fizzy drink. He'd taken only a couple of swigs before his name was called. In the anxiety of the moment, Caitlin left the drink behind on the seat of the waiting room.

Seeing an opportunity, another boy grabbed the bottle, unscrewed the top and wiped his right hand around it. He was about to finish off the drink, when his dad yelled at him. 'No! You don't know where it's been.'

He held up his hand. 'I wiped it.'

His father shook his head. 'Not enough. There'll be all sorts of germs in here. It's a hospital. Put it down. Come on. Your grandad'll be waiting.'

When the lad got to his grandfather's bedside in Ward D4, he decided to be all grown up. He held out his right hand like he'd seen his dad do lots of times.

Bill Garvey grinned, reached out weakly and shook it.

*

As soon as Finn walked into Karl's untidy bedroom, he said, 'I told you. They're out there looking for us!'

Karl didn't need to ask what his mate was talking about. 'Are you sure?'

Bouncer – despite appearances, a big softie – nudged Karl's hand till it came to rest on his head.

'I didn't recognise him, but he was one of them. He said he wanted to talk to us about what happened on Saturday.'

Karl stopped patting the dog. 'You spoke to him?'

'*He* spoke to *me*. Just before I pulled a runner. But here's the really bad news.'

'What?'

'He got my name. Adam's mum came past and said, "Hello, Finn."'

Karl took a deep breath. 'Only Finn? Not Pallister as well?'

'That's right.'

Karl looked relieved. 'Not too bad, then.'

'Oh, yeah? How many kids do you know called Finn?'

'Yeah, but without a last name, they can't look you up or anything.'

'It's all right for you. It wasn't your name they got. You're not up a gum tree without a paddle like me.'

'Come on. You got away. Crisis over.' Distracting Finn, Karl said, 'Bet you want to know what I've been up to while you were out walking Bouncer—'

Finn interrupted. 'And escaping from terrorists.'

'Yeah. I've been trying to translate a bit more of this.' Karl held up the pale blue notebook. 'She made it, you know, this *perrium* bacteria thingy. It's a new life form – like Frankenstein's monster, but smaller.'

'Didn't Frankenstein's monster go around killing people?'

Karl laughed. 'You're forgetting something.'

'What's that?'

'Frankenstein wasn't real.'

'Well,' Finn replied, twiddling his door key round his fingers, 'there's real blokes out there after us – especially me – because of her. Thanks a lot, Dr Can't-Cross-The-Road Perry.'

'I'm not sure about terrorists using her bug. It says here it can't attack people and she made a medicine for it anyway. It's safe. Even if someone got their hands on her notes and turned it into a nasty germ that went around killing people, you'd just give everyone this antidote.'

'Is that in the notes as well?'

Karl shook his head. 'It's in Notebook 7A. Bet that's up at the university, in her lab still.'

'Yeah, well. You'd better get outside and tell those three blokes it's no use tracking us down because I reckon they don't know their plan's rubbish.'

Karl hesitated. 'It's just that . . .'

'What?'

'I think Mr Dee said bacteria learn from each other. Bad ones could teach good ones new tricks. Dirty tricks.'

Finn sighed. 'Are you saying someone could screw things up if they got their hands on the instructions?'

'I'm not sure. Maybe.'

Finn looked genuinely downcast. 'I don't like germs. You should've seen Nan.' He shook his head. 'It was eating her up. Her leg got these black and smelly bumps. Like burnt sausages.' Normally, he would have revelled in gruesome facts but now he was dismayed. 'Horrible.'

On his way back from the kitchen, Karl hesitated in the living room, distracted by what was on the television. The camera lingered on a tall woman with a full bust beneath her low-cut top. Her hair was black, possibly dyed, and her ample make-up covered any wrinkles of the thirty-something. But it was the words of the programme's host that brought Karl to a halt.

With a serious face, the *Newsnight* presenter said, 'Following the tragic death of the biologist, Dr Eve Perry, at the weekend much has been said and written about scientists making life from scratch. I have with me Rosalind Monkhouse, Professor of Biology at the Communicable Disease Surveillance Centre, and the Archbishop of Liverpool, Patrick Owen. Archbishop, Dr Perry worked in your diocese and died very close to your cathedral. What's your attitude to your parishioner and her work?'

'First,' he answered, 'I want to express my sympathy for Dr Perry's parents. Every life is precious, of course, but because Dr Perry was young and so academically gifted, her loss is particularly sad. The fact that her work required such a brilliant mind tells me something, though. It proves that the creation of life can only come about through the intervention of considerable intelligence. Yet scientists are fond of telling us that, many years ago, nature assembled the first primitive life forms from dead things by chance and then random evolution turned them into today's sophisticated creatures. It's clear to me that a formidable intelligence must have brought life into the world. That guiding light,' he stressed, 'was God. Decisions about life and death started with Him and must be left to Him.'

Rosalind Monkhouse smiled as if she'd heard the argument before. 'If life only comes about through the intervention of an intelligent being, who made God? There's no evidence whatsoever for such a supernatural being.' She waved a hand – her fingers laden with rings and her wrist with bracelets – to dismiss the priest's views. 'You do need an exceptional biologist to tackle the making of new life, but that's because it takes the best brains to recreate what nature did millions of years ago. It breathed life into a soup of dead chemicals.'

'But,' the TV presenter asked, 'is it right for human beings to make a new species?'

'It depends on the reason,' Rosalind replied. 'It seems that Dr Perry had some ideas about using an artificial being – a bacterium – to reduce pollution and provide clean energy. All very worthy. She might also have answered some basic questions about the nature of life itself.'

She appeared to be relaxed and undaunted by the occasion. More than that, she seemed to be enjoying the limelight. Karl thought it was a pity that she didn't teach science at his school. She would have turned a lot more boys on to biology than Mr Dee ever could. If she'd been half her actual age, she would've had them queuing up for extra science.

'Is that right, Archbishop Owen? It's a good idea to create life if the rationale behind it is sound?'

'No. Basically, we've become too clever for our own good. Dr Perry was clearly talented but you have to appreciate that we are mere mortals and therefore not perfect. We've just heard from Professor Monkhouse that we don't really understand life. It's far too dangerous to meddle with something we don't understand – even for the best of motives. Only God has the wisdom to see the implications of creating a new species. Think about Genesis in the Bible. It's the story of people doing exactly what they knew they shouldn't do – like children. Told not to do something, the child wants to do it – just to see what happens. Somewhere deep down, we know it's not our place to create life but for some it seems the temptation's just too great.' He smiled wryly and added, 'With people, I'm afraid it's always forbidden fruit and serpents.'

The scientist shook her head theatrically. 'There are risks, of course. There's risk in everything we do. But there's a pay-off as well, and it could've been enormous. I'm sure an expert like Dr Perry would've contained the danger and exploited the benefits.'

Interrupting the programme, Karl's mum said, 'This is a first. Has your PlayStation packed up?'

'What do you mean?' asked Karl.

Mrs Stephenson laughed. 'Must be the first time you've taken an interest in newsy stuff like this.'

Karl held up the half-eaten Kit Kat. 'I only came down for a biscuit. But . . .' He waved it towards the telly. 'It's interesting. It happened in Brownlow Hill.'

'Oh? They didn't say so. How do you know?'

'I er . . . read it in the paper.'

'Reading the paper as well, now.'

Karl's dad said nothing. He was concentrating on the TV debate. Well, he was concentrating whenever Rosalind Monkhouse was in shot.

The presenter was firing his last questions. 'Was Dr Perry successful? Did she make a new creature and, if so, should we be simply curious or downright scared?'

Professor Monkhouse shrugged. 'We don't know if

she completed the project. Her notes have not come to light so I suspect we'll never know.'

As soon as the camera swung away from the glamorous biologist, Karl turned and went quickly back up to his room.

PART 2
OUTBREAK

CHAPTER 1

In Ward D4, Bill Garvey should have been getting better by the day. His heart bypass operation had been completely successful, giving him more get-up-and-go. But, all of a sudden, he wasn't going anywhere. Nurse Mollie Willett gazed at him with sympathy. 'You *do* look peaky today.'

Bill was managing to sit up in bed but he was very weak. His muscles ached and his chest felt heavy. Breathing had become a painful wheeze and his throat was on fire. And his tongue could tell that overnight something had gone drastically wrong inside his mouth. There were at least two new lumps and the horrible taste of blood. 'It's my mouth and throat,' he groaned.

'Can you open up and let me see?'

Mollie peered into his gaping mouth and did her best not to react with revulsion. She found herself looking into a filthy smelly cave with dark stalagmites and stalactites. The blisters poking up and hanging down were deep red to black and wet with saliva and blood. She cleared her own throat, gulped and stood back.

'You're right. You've got some swellings in there so I think we'll let the doctor have a look at you. It could be some sort of infection, but we'd better wait to see what the doctor says. Okay?'

The patient nodded pathetically.

'I'll go and give him a call, then I'll come back and check your blood pressure.'

Mollie went to the desk and poured her panic into the internal phone.

Even before sending a tissue sample to the pathology lab, Doctor Ali could make a diagnosis – and it wouldn't do the hospital's statistics any good at all. It looked like another clear case of hospital-acquired MRSA. Mr Garvey was weak after his operation and his immune system was not up to scratch so the bacteria were having a field day. Doctor Ali had no reason to believe that the infection was unique. He would realise that he was dealing with something unknown only forty-eight hours later when the lab results would hit him like a tornado.

For now, Doctor Ali didn't impose extra precautions. He simply reinforced the usual message about cleanliness to protect other patients. He didn't believe that there was any risk to the outside community. The MRSA bacterium was equipped to survive in cramped hospitals that provided a steady supply of vulnerable hosts. For MRSA, life inside was cushy. Out on the streets, where everyone was more-or-less healthy with fine immune systems, where there were too many competing bacteria, and where there were far fewer opportunities to spread around, the germs couldn't get a foothold.

At the end of the shift, the hospital allowed Nurse Mollie Willett to go home without another thought.

Shaughney Willett knew it was her duty, as a teenage daughter, to fight with her mother every step of the way. That's what all her mates did. But Shaughney was different. She actually *liked* her mum. Maybe they didn't clash because, after a ferocious stint of fighting ill health and sometimes an all-night shift, her mum had no energy for fighting her daughter as well. That gave Shaughney free range on clothes, make-up, jewellery and staying out times.

That Thursday evening, her mum – still in her nurse's uniform – sank into an armchair and let out a long weary breath. Shaughney looked at her and, instead of asking what was for tea, said, 'Blimey. You look like you've just done double maths with the world's most boring teacher.'

'A double lesson? Make that an entire term, then you're getting close.'

Shaughney smiled. 'Not a good day, I take it.'

'Don't ask. You don't want to know. And you certainly don't want a description. That'd put you off your tea.'

'Talking of tea . . .'

Mollie groaned. 'I can't face making it. We'll splash out. I'll give you the money for fish and chips. Not that I feel much like eating.'

'Must be bad.'

Mollie held her arm out. 'Here. Give us a pull-up.'

Shaughney stopped fiddling with an earring, grabbed her mother's limp hand and yanked her upright.

On Friday, Angus Kerven was loitering outside Archbishop Benedict School near the top of Brownlow Hill, carefully watching the students at going-home time. Making up his mind, he picked out a girl who appeared to be about the same age as Finn. She was a deliberate choice. Angus was powerfully built and handsome with it. He'd never had trouble impressing the opposite sex, especially the younger ones. 'Sorry to bother you . . .' he began.

She had short fair hair, almost the pale yellow colour of straw. She was tilting her head to one side as she fitted a giant hoop earring that probably wasn't allowed in school. She gazed at his face, looked him up and down, then replied, 'No bother.'

'I'm looking for Finn. Have you seen him? He asked me to meet him here.'

'Finn?' She shrugged as she attached the other earring and the schoolbag slipped off her shoulder.

Angus stepped forward, picked it up and held it out for her.

The girl looked at him, took the bag and muttered, 'Thanks.'

Angus put his hand in front of his mouth and stubbly chin while he cleared his throat. 'Yeah. Finn with the Alsatian.'

The young woman shook her head and the earrings collided with her shoulders. 'Sorry. Never heard of him.' With a cheeky grin, she added, 'Pity I can't help you.'

That was Kerven's third attempt to trace the boy who'd taken Perry's lab book. And his third blank. But he hadn't lost faith in the tactic. The goal of retrieving the notes was too important to give up easily. Next week, he'd try the kids pouring out of the other schools in the area.

Shaughney had little but contempt for boys of her own age. She preferred more mature types like the good-looking guy who had asked her about a lad called Finn. He was rugged, late twenties, and he must have worked out to keep his body in that sort of shape. On her sliding scale, she marked him eighty-five per cent on the way to Brad Pitt. But, while she liked what she saw, she had to be suspicious about a bloke hanging out at the school gates and asking fishy questions. She wasn't going to tell a stranger that every Monday evening someone called Finn went to the Brontë Youth and Community Centre for the Teen and Toddler Scheme.

She grabbed her schoolbag from him, shook her head and shrugged. 'Sorry. Never heard of him.' That wasn't true, of course, but she didn't really know Finn so the lie wasn't an unforgivable sin. Still, it was a shame to turn her back on this man. She smiled sweetly. 'Pity I can't help you.'

At once, Grace dashed up to her and said, 'Who was that?'

'Oh, you know. Just another bloke trying to pick me up.'

'Yeah, sure.' Grace hesitated, then asked, 'Did he?'

Shaughney laughed. 'Great body, gorgeous, but not quite up to the mark for me. Besides, he was asking after that lad called Finn.'

'The one at the Teens and Toddlers? The one whose mate fancies you?'

'I suppose so.'

'Why?'

Shaughney shrugged and sent her earrings into convulsions. 'He seemed to think this is Finn's school. Said Finn had arranged to meet him here.'

'That doesn't make sense,' Grace replied.

'No. Not unless he was trying to con me for some reason.'

'Oh?'

Shaughney sniffed. 'I'm working on a theory.'

The girls waited for a bus to rumble past, belching blue smoke, before crossing the road. 'What's that, then?' said Grace.

'Well, you know that woman who died down the bottom of the hill on Saturday?'

'No.'

'Yes, you do. The one the teachers have been going on about, talking like she was the devil for trying to produce a new species. Like God was driving the car that hit her.'

'Oh, her. What's she got to do with it?'

'It was in the paper,' Shaughney said. 'The police are after two boys that ran away from the accident. White, teenage, average height and build. One with short fair hair and the other with long dark hair.'

'So?'

Shaughney smiled slyly. 'It got me thinking when I read it. Doesn't it remind you of anyone? It did me.'

Grace hesitated for a moment, then said, 'You think it's Finn and the other one. And the chap outside school was a plain-clothes cop.'

'In hot pursuit, maybe.'

'Wouldn't he have shown you your ID or something?'

'Dunno. Not if he was undercover.'

'What are you going to do about it?'

Shaughney took a big breath. 'Not a lot.'

'I think we should go and warn them.'

Shaughney turned to her friend with a big grin. 'I know why you want to go. You fancy him!'

'Who?'

'Finn.'

Grace denied it. 'No, I don't.'

'Why would your cheeks put a beetroot to shame, then?'

CHAPTER 2

It wasn't a job for Sherlock Holmes. Shaughney and Grace simply called in at the Brontë Youth and Community Centre and asked the supervisor. It turned out that both boys lived in the dreary prison block opposite the Catholic cathedral. Outside, they ran into Adam Satchwell who was trying to escape from his watchful mother. He was about to fall over onto the pavement when Shaughney reached down and grabbed both of his little hands. He giggled, pulled his arms away from her, shoved one thumb in his mouth and tottered back towards his mum. Recognising the girls, Caitlin nodded and said, 'Hi.'

Shaughney and Grace returned the greeting as they walked past and into the building. Their knock at the door of Finn's ground-floor flat set off a dog. It sounded gruff and loud.

Eventually Finn appeared in the doorway, holding back a dog by its collar. He looked stunned to see the girls. 'You're from . . .' He jerked his head in the direction of the youth centre.

Leaning against the door-frame, Shaughney nodded. 'Yeah – and we've come to do you a favour.'

Now Finn looked downright puzzled. 'How do you mean?'

The dog – an Alsatian, just as the dishy bloke had said – came forward to sniff Shaughney's leg. She patted its head. 'Hello. What's your name, then?'

'Bouncer,' Finn answered.

She smiled. 'He looks the part, but he's not exactly fierce, is he?'

'What's this favour?' Finn asked, looking from Shaughney to Grace and back again.

Prolonging his agony, Shaughney said, 'We know your little secret.'

'What?'

'You and your mate – and the new-life woman.'

If Shaughney had been wrong, Finn would have been baffled. But he wasn't. He swallowed and then said, 'Ah.'

'Well?' Shaughney prompted.

'Er . . . Let's go to Karl's,' Finn replied. 'He's up on the fourth floor.' He pushed the Alsatian back into the flat and made for the stairs.

Behind him, Shaughney complained, 'Why aren't we using the lift?'

'The lift?' Finn grimaced and shook his head. 'You don't want to go in there, even when it's working.' He screwed up his nose to indicate a nasty smell.

Twice on the way up, Finn glanced nervously over his shoulder.

'Relax,' Shaughney told him. 'The police don't know which school you go to. And I don't think they know your surname.'

'The police?'

'Mmm.'

Finn stopped midway up the third flight. 'Are you talking about a bloke, six foot tall, shortish dark hair, big build, drives a Toyota?'

Shaughney nodded. 'I don't know about his car. Broad shoulders, good-looking, blue eyes.'

'Yes, he drove away in a Toyota,' said Grace. Then she touched her chin with her hand. 'Quite a bit of stubble as well.'

Finn nodded. 'He's got nothing to do with the police. More like the opposite.' He turned and carried on towards Karl's place.

Intrigued, Shaughney followed with Grace.

When Karl opened the door and saw his three visitors, his expression ranged from shock, to embarrassment, to delight. His hand darted to his mass of dark curls, making a futile attempt to neaten them. Watching him, Shaughney could not keep a grin off her face.

Karl's bedroom was a mess, dominated by a PlayStation, an Everton poster, and several pictures of racing cars and female singers revealing as much skin as possible without actually being indecent. There wasn't a single bookshelf in the whole place. It looked as if he'd got only one book and that wasn't a proper paperback. It was a thick notepad of some sort. Hastily, Karl covered his crinkled sheet with the duvet. That seemed to be the extent of his bed-making and it was about as effective as brushing his tousled hair with his hand. Shaughney and Grace sat on the crumpled surface, propped against the wall, while the two boys lounged on the floor.

After Shaughney explained what had happened outside their school, Finn and Karl exchanged looks as if trying to decide what to do without actually speaking to each other.

Just as Shaughney tended to talk for the girls, Karl became the boys' spokesman. 'Yeah, well, thanks for telling us, but the guy's no cop.'

'How do you know?' asked Shaughney.

Karl glanced again at his mate before spilling out an almost unbelievable tale about a chase through the city, laboratory notes, terrorists and bugs that ate pollution. But Shaughney had to believe some of it because Karl showed her the biological notebook. He kept tight hold of it, though, as if it were too precious to hand over to someone else. Leaning forward to read a couple of pages, Shaughney and Grace realised that it was genuine. It was gibberish to them but it would be important jargon to someone in the know. According to these boys, it could be a bioterrorist's instruction manual.

Shaughney thought about it for a few seconds. 'Well, I'm not a brilliant professor or anything but I reckon there's a glaring hole in all of this. You said she was keeping her new beast under lock-and-key in her lab, but she wanted it to soak up carbon dioxide. It couldn't do that unless she let it loose into the big, wide world.'

'I wondered about that as well,' Karl said. He flicked through the pages near the end of the notebook. 'There's a section here somewhere on air purification. Says something about a cabinet that won't let her bacteria out but lets air in. Used air's pumped in, the bugs munch the carbon dioxide and environment-friendly air comes out.'

Shaughney was surprised. If this boy could make even partial sense of it, he was more intelligent than he looked. 'Sounds more like a nice little earner than a threat. I bet it's business people – not terrorists – trying to muscle in on a money-spinner.'

Looking at Finn, Grace asked, 'What are you going to do?'

He shrugged helplessly.

From upstairs, the relentless thud of rap began. Caught by surprise, Shaughney muttered, 'Blimey.' Then she coughed. Her throat and tongue felt dry and unpleasantly tickly. 'Well, it's got nothing to do with us. We just came to warn you.'

'We're not going to the police,' Karl said. 'This bloke's mates will be watching out for us.'

'The cops'll do us for taking the book – even though the woman wanted us to,' Finn added.

Karl nodded. 'They'll say we nicked it. And they'll have us for leaving the scene of an accident as well.'

'Please yourselves.' Shaughney stood up.

Karl looked disappointed. 'Oh. Are you going?' He paused timidly before adding, 'Do you want to . . . er . . .'

'What?'

'Nothing. Doesn't matter.'

Grace smiled and nodded at Finn.

Seeing her friend's expression of interest in Finn, Shaughney decided to take pity on her and make a sacrifice. She turned back to Karl and said, 'Yeah, all right.'

'What?'

'You were going to ask us out. We'll come and see you tomorrow afternoon. Won't we, Grace?'

Karl's face was transparent again. He positively beamed. Trying to get his feelings under control, he said, 'Okay. That'd be cool.' He still didn't manage to sound laid-back, though.

Finn merely looked like a lad who was going to have to miss the football.

*

Towards the bottom end of Brownlow Hill, bunches of flowers were attached to a lamppost. The sight of the tribute to Dr Perry brought the four of them to a halt. Finn kept his eye on the road, no doubt on the lookout for a Toyota. He seemed more attentive to cars than to Grace. Shaughney checked out the bouquets, then said mischievously, 'Nothing from the church.'

It was a weird foursome on the way to Liverpool's waterfront. Only two – Grace and Karl – were keen on the idea, though not on each other. Shaughney was bored already. Thinking of the dead scientist, she decided to spice up the flagging conversation. 'You know, a kid comes with responsibility.' Glancing at Bouncer, she added, 'Like a pet dog. That's what the Teen and Toddler Scheme's all about. Kids aren't just for Christmas.'

'Yeah,' Karl replied, 'but what's that got to do with Eve Perry's bug?' He almost whispered.

'She brought it into the world. No wonder she's called Eve. It's like her kiddie.'

'Yeah, well, she's not here to look after it any more.'

'That's right. She sort-of made you its guardian, didn't she? Right here where she died. That's what you said. She gave you its birth certificate. You're step-dad to a bug.'

'I suppose . . .' Karl muttered.

'Let's get going,' Finn said, shuffling from foot to foot.

'Scared someone might recognise your description?' Shaughney replied with a sly smile. 'Feel like a baddie returning to the scene of the crime?'

'Maybe,' Finn answered.

The girls tanked up on cider outside the Pumphouse looked like they were having a good time. A much better time than Shaughney, anyway. She watched Finn pick up a couple of stones and lob them into the Mersey. She had no idea why boys always did that. And she doubted that it was impressing Grace. At least Karl wasn't joining in. Even Finn's Alsatian was bored with the action. Bouncer showed much more interest in the local smells than taking a dip in a doomed attempt to retrieve the stones. The dog had more sense than its owner.

'What do you think of the Teen and Toddler thing?' Shaughney asked.

Karl shrugged. 'It's okay.'

'Why did you join?'

'Well . . . You know.' There was colour in his cheeks as he failed to find an answer.

Shaughney laughed aloud. 'I bet you did it to meet girls! How sad can you get?'

'What about you, then?'

'Come on! We go to Archbishop Benedict's. Catholic. Sex education is, "Don't do it!" Seeing a lot of babies is supposed to reinforce the message.' Then, for fun,

Shaughney decided to embarrass the boys. 'No sex, no babies, no condoms.'

She should have realised that it was impossible to embarrass Finn. 'It's better at our school,' he blurted out. 'We got to put a condom on a cucumber.'

Straightaway, Karl added, 'That's why the world isn't overrun with cucumbers.'

A wicked grin on her face, Shaughney replied, 'It would've been better to practise on asparagus.'

Not understanding the insult, Finn shrugged. He'd never seen a spindly asparagus.

'When you think about it,' Shaughney added, 'our lot don't want science to stop new life and they don't want it to start new life either.'

Always more serious than her friend, Grace said, 'I think there's a difference between having kids and making a new species.'

Out of habit, Finn was pressing his door key first into one palm and then into the other. He looked up and said, 'We've got sniffer dogs on the way in to our school.'

It was clear to Shaughney that God had committed a howler when He came to wiring Finn's brain. She imagined that Grace found his innocence endearing.

There was a moment of silence before a bamboozled Grace asked, 'To sniff out condoms?'

'No. Drugs.'

If Finn hadn't already killed the conversation,

Shaughney's mobile finished it off altogether. It was her mum, telling her that there was a problem at the hospital. A big problem. She needed to see her daughter. Now.

CHAPTER 3

Nurse Willett had drawn the curtain right around the hospital bed. Bill Garvey was centre stage but the audience had been excluded. That way, his appearance wouldn't upset visitors and the other patients. His mouth was too full of infected tissue to close or to cope with food so he took his nutrition continuously via a drip. Through his open mouth, he dragged air into his inflamed lungs, absorbed precious oxygen, and breathed out waste carbon dioxide. He could no longer use his nose. It had exploded with the pressure of the swellings inside his nostrils. A scan had shown that his lungs were also heavily contaminated with the rapidly multiplying microbe.

In disbelief, Doctor Ali read the pathology results again, shaking his head. 'Well, it's not MRSA. It might be a strange version of it but . . .' He sighed. 'The lab's never seen it before.' He could speak freely because Bill Garvey was no longer conscious, but the medic kept his voice down so the world beyond the curtain could not hear. 'Because it's not MRSA, it might succumb to drugs. Pathology's testing antibiotics on cultures of it

71

right now. Till we get an answer, keep him comfortable and give him vancomycin.'

'What about us?' Mollie asked quietly, even though she felt like screaming.

'This isn't a crisis situation. It's only one patient,' the medic replied. 'We won't know about its virulence till we get more results from the lab. My guess is, it'll only be rampant in the old, sick and the very young – like MRSA. So, make sure everyone washes their hands between patients. And I think the ward needs to pay more attention to visitors. I'm not convinced they all use the antibacterial wipes.'

Back at home, Shaughney had barely got through the door when her mother asked, 'How are you feeling?'

'Great. You saved us from some deadly boring boys.'

'Be sensible, Shaughney.'

'There's plenty of time for me to be sensible when I'm old – like you.'

Her mum was plainly not in the mood. 'I meant your health.'

Shaughney looked surprised. She shrugged. 'Fine.'

'How about your mouth and throat?'

'Mum!'

'No, Shaughney. This is serious. Tell me.'

'All right,' she said as she got out of her coat. 'Maybe I've got a bit of a sore throat, but it's nothing. Sore's not the word, really. It's a bit tingly, that's all. Don't come all Mother Theresa on me.'

'Let me see.'

Shaughney backed away under protest. 'What? Why? I'm fifteen, Mum, not five.'

'A germ's a germ, five or fifteen.'

'It's March. Runny noses and sore throats are all the rage.'

'I'm still going to take a look.'

Shaughney sighed loudly. But she could see that her mother was stressed and determined. She threw her coat onto a chair and put her fists on her waist. 'All right, doc. If it makes you happy.' She opened her mouth like a bad-tempered and hungry shark. 'Get it over with.'

Her mum peered inside as if she were looking for a blockage in a dark drain. 'Mmm. Seems to be okay. I can't see anything.'

'Really!' Shaughney cried, feigning panic. 'So where have all my teeth gone?'

Not even a flicker of a smile. 'Nothing *untoward*,' her mum stressed. 'Thank God.'

'What's this all about?'

'You really don't want to know. Just a one-off infection, I hope. But ... Just promise you'll tell me straightaway if anyone you know starts coughing and spluttering – or complaining about a sore throat or mouth. Okay?'

Shaughney shrugged. 'It's the season for colds, but . . . If you say so.'

'Promise.'

'Blimey. Yes, all right. Promise.' As soon as her mother turned her back, Shaughney feigned a loud coughing fit.

Her mum spun round and yelled, 'Not funny!'

The first girl looked distrustfully at Kerven and muttered, 'Piss off.' The second seemed to be about to kick him on the shin but she didn't. Instead, she ran back to a group of friends. No doubt she was whispering something about the peculiar man standing outside Kingsway School.

Kerven had better luck with his third choice. 'Excuse me,' he said. 'I'm looking for Finn. Have you seen him?'

'Finn Pallister?'

Angus was feeling dire. His head was stuffed-up and his breath short. Still, the aches and pains helped him to keep a self-satisfied smile off his face. 'Yes.'

'Who wants to know?'

'His mum sent me . . .'

'You're too late. He left early. Said he wasn't feeling good.'

It was plain from the girl's expression that she didn't believe Finn's excuse for missing school on Monday afternoon. Kerven managed a grin. 'Yeah, that sounds like Finn all right. Do you know where he went?'

'No.'

He couldn't ask where Finn lived because he was supposed to be a friend of the family who would have known Finn's address. 'Whereabouts does he hang out when he's bunking off?'

The girl shrugged. 'No idea, but you could try him tonight at the Community Centre, Teen and Toddler Scheme.'

'Good idea. Thanks.' Kerven's hand over his mouth hid a smirk as he walked away. It also muffled his coughing.

Sheltered from a bitter wind, Shaughney stood against the concrete wall, watching the toddlers arriving with their mums. The youngsters in buggies with all-over clear plastic coverings reminded her of goldfish. Some tottered slowly under their own steam, wrapped up in layers of clothing. Others were bundled up in their mothers' arms like rugs. Shaughney nodded a greeting as each one came past and entered the Youth and Community Centre. Her earrings felt cold against her neck.

Little Adam ran towards the door with arms out and a huge grin. His movement wasn't exactly elegant. He looked like a miniature drunk struggling to keep control of his wayward legs as he staggered forwards. Shaughney wondered what her mum would make of Adam and the other toddlers. Half of them seemed to be sniffling and sneezing. She'd promised to shop them for the sin of having colds. But she wasn't going to, because it was silly.

A new arrival by the road made her gasp. Spotting the man who had quizzed her at the school gates on Friday, she nudged Grace and whispered, 'It's him. See?'

Grace glanced at him and then shrank behind her friend.

'Look,' Shaughney said. 'They're multiplying.'

Fiddling with the crucifix around her neck as if it would protect her, Grace took a peek. Now there were three men on the pavement, talking quietly to each other. One was stocky and black, the other two were taller and white. One was well built and the other wiry in comparison. All three were in their twenties or thirties. They showed no sign of seeing or recognising Shaughney. They seemed more intent on scheming between themselves.

'They don't look like dads with toddlers,' Shaughney muttered.

'They give me a bad feeling. What should we do?'

'Warn Karl and Finn, I suppose.'

'They're not here yet.'

Shaughney nodded. 'Any second now, so let's intercept them at their place.'

'All right.'

The three men had dispersed. They were probably circling the building.

Before jogging over the road, Grace said, 'Just a minute.' She looked round nervously and then knelt down by the parked Toyota. Quickly, she unscrewed the dust cap on the front nearside wheel. While Shaughney kept watch, she pressed her little fingernail onto the needle of the valve. At once, the air hissed loudly as the tyre quickly deflated.

Shaughney laughed. 'And here's me thinking you were a good Catholic girl!'

Grace stood up and said, 'At least, they won't be able to chase Finn in the car.'

They hurried into the block of flats and took up a position by the stairs. They didn't have to wait for long. Within a minute, the two boys emerged from Finn's apartment.

Straightaway, Shaughney said, 'I've got some bad news for you . . .'

Behind them, the door had opened. The good-looking guy said, 'And I've got some more. That wasn't my Toyota.'

All four of them stared at him.

'Thanks,' he said to Shaughney. 'You led me here very nicely . . .'

Karl exclaimed, 'Bugger!' With Finn, he took off along the gloomy corridor in the opposite direction.

This time, the industrial spy, terrorist, cop or whatever he was didn't seem so dishy. He looked pasty and tired, unsteady, hardly capable of breaking into a sprint. Even so, that's what he tried to do. As he pushed his way unceremoniously past the girls, Shaughney kicked out at his ankle and he spilled onto the floor. She exchanged a grin with Grace, but her good mood soon vanished. The chap sprawled on the tiled floor didn't get up and curse Shaughney. He just lay there, uncannily still.

Worried, Shaughney tiptoed round him, half expecting him to grab her leg angrily at any moment. But he didn't. She squatted down near his head. His eyes were closed and his mouth open. A little blood was leaking from between his teeth onto the broken tiles. She looked up at Grace sheepishly.

'What have you done?' Grace stammered.

'Nothing. Just a harmless . . .' She peered again at his face. Thick crimson fluid was also dribbling from his nose and the gaping hole of a mouth did not look right. She didn't have to be a nurse like her mother to know that a blackened and bloody tongue spelled trouble.

She got to her feet and backed away from him. Horrified, her heart thudding, she mumbled, 'Something's wrong here.'

CHAPTER 4

To Shaughney and Grace, the hospital's waiting room felt like a cemetery – a space that divided the living from the dead. The atmosphere was hushed and dreary. Shaughney's mum had told them to expect a nurse who would take a blood sample for analysis and a doctor who'd examine them and ask a few questions.

'This man you found,' Doctor Ali said as he peered like a potholer down Grace's throat using a small powerful torch. 'Do you know him?'

Grace's tongue was pinned down by a spatula so Shaughney answered. 'No.'

The doctor was skinny, shorter than Shaughney, and he wore unfashionable heavy-framed glasses. 'You don't know his name?'

'No.' Shaughney hesitated, then added, 'But *you* would if you searched his pockets.'

Doctor Ali shook his head and moved on to Shaughney. 'He wasn't carrying any ID.'

'He drives a Toyota,' Grace said.

The medic glanced from Shaughney's mouth back to Grace. 'Do you know its registration number?'

'Sorry.'

'Did either of you touch him?'

Shaughney didn't count an ankle tap as touching. 'No.'

The doctor stepped back and switched off his little lamp. 'You both look fine for the moment. Wait here and, just to make sure, we'll do some blood tests.'

'Is he . . . all right?' Grace asked. 'The man we found.'

Doctor Ali took a deep breath. 'We're doing what we can for him.'

'That means no,' Shaughney said.

The medic didn't reply but his tired eyes behind the lenses told her that she was right.

Doctor Ali found himself on a level with the considerable bust of the glamorous expert from the Communicable Disease Surveillance Centre. Towering over him, Professor Rosalind Monkhouse introduced herself. He held out his hand but she didn't take it at once. Instead, she said, 'Have you used an antibacterial wash?'

'Yes.'

'In that case . . .'

Her bracelets jangled and he felt her many rings against his skin as she shook his hand. 'I guess you want to see the patients right away,' he said.

'No.'

'But . . .'

'My assistant takes care of that end of the business.'

A young man – hardly more than a student and looking even younger – stepped forward. 'Damian Brack,' he said. 'I'll examine them.'

'After we've moved some equipment in,' Rosalind added.

'I hope it won't take long,' Doctor Ali replied, looking up into her face. 'I called you in because, whatever the bacterium is, it's doubling its numbers every twenty minutes.'

'From what you said on the phone, your first patient's not going to pull through. Damian's likely to be working on post-mortem material.' Her matter-of-fact tone was devoid of sentiment but her eyes hinted of pain.

Doctor Ali lowered his gaze. 'And . . . er, if you don't mind me asking, what do you do?'

'I'm going to beat your bug by thinking, by working out a long-term solution,' Rosalind replied. 'Damian will worry about patients, I'll worry about the community at large, the bigger picture. And, I guess, make myself a thorough nuisance with the hospital management.'

The Teen and Toddler session was turning into a disaster. Four of the teens – Shaughney Willett, Grace Fordham, Karl Stephenson and Finn Pallister – hadn't shown up, even though the two girls had been seen outside the centre. A mother who volunteered her twins for the scheme was seething because someone had let down one of her front tyres. She was threatening not to come again. And she reported that two men seemed to be prowling around outside. Several of the toddlers were coughing and sneezing. There weren't even enough young people to wipe their runny noses and keep them clean. The mums sat in the tearoom and, with increasingly concerned faces, compared their children's symptoms.

When one of the part-time carers put his head round the door and said he'd seen a little blood mixed with the mucus, alarm bells really started to ring.

Curtis Bennett agreed to stay with Smith and patrol the youth centre while Kerven – on a hunch – followed the girl with the shiny red hoop earrings. Curtis knew why their ruthless leader usually stayed close to him during operations. Weston Smith regarded him as unstable because of his frustration and nerves. Well, what could he expect? Curtis wasn't cut out for this line of work. He was a scientist. Or rather a penniless ex-scientist. Smith and Kerven couldn't drop him, though, because they needed his knowledge of science and scientists.

Maybe the two extremists also suspected him. Curtis hoped not, but he feared the worst because he wasn't good at acting. He was scared of what would happen if they found out about him and his real agenda. Smith could be cold-blooded and brutal in pursuit of the group's aims. And it wasn't just a play on words that gave Angus Kerven the nickname of Angry.

The flow of people into the Brontë Youth and Community Centre had run dry and the two boys hadn't appeared. Smith's sneaky look inside the building told them that they weren't inside either. On top of that, Angry hadn't returned.

Before long, there was a mass exodus from the concrete monstrosity. A few of the mums and toddlers headed up the road in the direction of the Royal Liverpool University Hospital. They looked like the dregs of a defeated army on the move. Curtis didn't know what was going on. Maddeningly, he was no nearer to Eve Perry's laboratory notes. Still, there was one bright spot. Angry had told them that he believed one of the boys who ran off with her lab book was called Finn Pallister. A name gave them something to work on.

CHAPTER 5

Shaughney and Grace found Finn in Karl's flat. The two boys seemed subdued and the place was quiet. Bouncer didn't let out a bark, growl or a whimper. The PlayStation remained dormant and mercifully the guy upstairs was either out or he'd blown a fuse on his sound system. 'What happened to you?' Shaughney asked them.

'Vanished for a bit. That's all,' Karl answered.

'Just as well we're good at it,' Finn added, stroking his four-legged minder. His usual grin had been dulled by feelings of vulnerability.

Karl glanced through the window. 'No one following you this time?'

'He's not up to following anyone any more,' Shaughney replied.

Talking to the boys, Grace said, 'She nearly murdered him so you could get away.'

'I only tripped him up.'

'Where is he now?' Karl said.

'Hospital,' Shaughney replied.

'Good,' Finn mumbled. 'One down, two to go.'

84

'Not very sympathetic,' said Shaughney with a smile. Then she looked at Karl. 'Have you still got that notebook they're after?'

'Yes,' Karl answered, glancing towards a cupboard.

'Does it say anything about throats and mouths by any chance?'

'Not that I've seen. What's that got to do with it?'

Shaughney shrugged. 'Probably nothing.'

The invasion of the hospital's paediatric unit by toddlers and anxious mums took the staff by surprise. The children's department hadn't yet heard about the trouble brewing in Ward D4 so the medics didn't take extra care. They carried out routine checks on the babies, took a few samples, and reassured the neurotic mothers. Behind the scenes, they talked about mass hysteria and nodded knowingly. Then they sent all of the toddlers home.

But the next day, Caitlin Satchwell was back. Her little boy was weak, coughing blood, and suffering chest pain. Caitlin herself was frantic.

Word had now got around the entire hospital that an expert from the Communicable Disease Surveillance Centre had arrived. Rumour had it that there were two worrying instances of infections and that they threatened to dominate the hospital's business. Everyone knew that Ward D4 had been closed to visitors and ordinary patients.

When the paediatric doctor on duty examined Adam and requested a consultation with the expert, she got someone called Damian Brack. He must have been in his twenties but he appeared barely older than the teens who'd looked after the toddlers at the youth centre. He examined Adam's mouth and nose and demanded a scan of his lungs. This Damian then fast-tracked all of the samples taken from the toddlers yesterday and admitted Adam Satchwell to Ward D4 where he would be isolated.

Upstaged by someone who looked like an inexperienced student, the paediatric doctor became tetchy, mistaking Damian for an insignificant assistant. Little did she realise that Damian was actually the bravest person in the Royal Liverpool University Hospital at that moment.

In front of a hastily assembled team, Professor Rosalind Monkhouse took a deep breath. 'This bacterium,' she began, 'isn't our usual enemy: the hospital-bound multi-drug-resistant MRSA. I don't know what it *is* yet, but it's a new kid on the block – a leaner, meaner killing machine almost certainly brought in from the community. It's out-competing the old lumbering superbug but it seems to have all MRSA's hostility and ruthlessness. And our first three patients – a toddler, a pensioner and a man in his twenties – tell us it doesn't care about the age of its victims. Even though there are more unknowns than facts at this stage, I'll promise you this: they won't be our only cases.

'For now, all we can do is surgery, little more than butchery. We're going to cut out the infected tissue, then use every antibiotic we can get our hands on to stop the bacteria getting another stranglehold.' She gazed at the hospital manager and continued, 'I want all leave for surgeons and resuscitation teams cancelled. And you're going to have to sign up every plastic surgeon in the area. If necessary, bully them into working here. There's going to be a lot for them to do after the surgeons have done their stuff. And I think the bacteria are going to push a lot of patients into shock. Blood pressure will drop like lead and organs will fail one by one. The shock teams won't be able to bring some of those people back. We're going to have fatalities – possibly lots of them. Bill Garvey will be the first.'

The room was totally silent as Rosalind spoke. 'No one's going to come to work in uniform because they could bring bacteria in on the material. No one's leaving in uniform either, in case they take this infection home with them. So, all work clothing stays on site and the hospital provides laundry services. I dare say we'll have to buy in a lot more gear to cope. Every member of the medical staff has got to start their shift in sterile clothes. That means management has got to set aside hygienic changing facilities for the nurses. And we need a twenty-four/seven cleaning team controlled by a matron.' Before the manager could raise an objection based on expense, Rosalind said, 'Remember, all this is a lot cheaper than the lives it'll cost if we don't do it.'

She barely paused for breath. 'The bacteria are targeting the mouth, nose and throat. So, keep your hands – and anything else that could possibly be contaminated – well away from your faces. I'll give all nursing staff a crash refresher course on infection control, and put procedures in place for reporting incidents where containment's compromised.' She leaned forward and some of her bracelets clunked on the tabletop. 'This isn't a time to cover up mistakes. It's a time for minimising the damage our mistakes cause. Everyone tells me if they have slip-ups. Right?'

Nearly everybody in the team was already in uniform, all set to swing into action. The hospital manager had a type of uniform as well: pinstripe suit and tie. Professor Monkhouse was dressed and made up as if she were on her way to a dinner party. Entirely inappropriate for making life-and-death decisions. But she was a formidable figure – both intellectually and physically.

She leaned back again. 'Now, let's get something out of the way right here. Sooner or later – probably sooner – some of you are going to accuse me of being the general who stays safely at home while ordering the troops to the frontline. There's a couple of reasons you won't see me much on the battlefield. If I'm going to see this thing through, I can't go down with it.' Then she patted the slight bulge at her belly that no one had noticed. 'What's more, I'm pregnant and I won't put my unborn child at risk. It wouldn't be fair to him or her – and I'd be an irresponsible mother – if I did anything that resulted in Junior getting exposed to this infection. Obviously, I can only protect my baby by protecting myself. If anyone's got any issues with that, you'd better say so right now.'

The stunned silence persisted.

Rosalind smiled. 'Nothing to say? Not even congratulations?'

Her light-hearted comment broke the spell at last.

'We might all be getting exposed to it right now – just by being here,' Nurse Willett said.

Professor Monkhouse nodded. 'Possibly, but unlikely. That's why I asked you all to scrub up before you came in here. I've got a hotel room down the road and there'll be a video link before the end of the day. But if this thing's in the community already – as I suspect it is – none of us is really safe unless we emigrate to the Seychelles. And sooner or later a tourist would import it there as well.'

'Shouldn't you be putting Liverpool under quarantine if it's that serious?' Doctor Ali asked.

'What? Close Liverpool? We'd have to stop every car, train, boat and plane. You can't block all movement in and out, every road and path, every person, every animal. I'm going to work out how it's going from person to person, but what we need first and foremost is a cure.' She paused before adding, 'Which brings me to something else I need to get in the open: everyone's attitude to Damian. Don't be fooled by his age. He's good. He's not with us at the moment because he's at the front, putting himself in more danger than anyone else, like a soldier clearing landmines. There are plenty of other places he could be – safe places – but he volunteered to come here and help. I know you'll bear all this in mind when you deal with him. He has my full authority at all times.

'Now, I want to know if anyone's got any ideas on what links our first three cases. I don't care how far-fetched you think it is. I just want ideas.'

'Er . . .'

'It's Mollie, isn't it?' Rosalind asked the nurse who was trying to find the right words.

'Yes. Nurse on Ward D4. I'm sorry but I think it might be me – and my daughter.'

'Oh yes?'

'I took care of Mr Garvey, my daughter came across the second man and she goes to the Teen and Toddler Scheme down the road. The same one as Adam Satchwell.'

'Have the two of you been tested?'

Mollie answered, 'Both negative.'

'Okay. Good. It doesn't tell us how Bill Garvey got it

in the first place, but it's a starting point. I'll get Damian to visit your house when he's got a minute. He'll talk to your daughter and all her contacts – especially this Teen and Toddler group – and take some samples for the path lab to look at.' She stood up and clapped her manicured hands twice. 'Right. Thanks, everybody. Let's get moving.'

CHAPTER 6

She looked like she was sound asleep. Asleep but not in bed at home. It was three days after Damian Brack's fifth birthday and he was tempted to pull the pillow out from under his mummy's head and bash her playfully with it. She'd jump up, growl like a tiger – as if she was mad at him – and then begin to laugh. She'd wallop him with the other pillow or throw it at him. Then he'd get a hug.

Grasping the bedding, Damian's head was level with his sleeping mother. But she wasn't sleeping. She was doing something called dying. And she was doing it in hospital. Damian didn't understand. It was like a sleep that lasted for ever. She'd never have another pillow fight with him, never throw him a ball, never make his tea or give him a bath. She'd never read to him while he went to sleep. Never ever.

'Wake up,' he whispered to her.

It was Daddy's hand on his shoulder and Daddy was crying for the very first time.

'Make her wake up, Daddy.'

Daddy dropped onto his knees and shook his head. 'I can't.'

'But I want you to.'

'I would if I could.'

'Why can't you?'

'Because ... Mummy's too sick to get better. She's ...'

Damian thumped his father on the chest. 'I want her, not you!' He turned away, grabbed a handful of blanket and shouted, 'Wake up!'

From behind, Granny took him and wrapped him up in her big arms. 'Let her rest, Damian. She's ... tired.'

'No. I want my mummy.' He hit the bed with his little fists and burst into tears.

He was angry with Daddy for not doing anything about it, angry with Granny for not being his mother, and especially angry with Mummy for going into a forever sleep and leaving him.

Damian didn't know it in 1985 but he was also angry with methicillin-resistant *Staphylococcus aureus* – dubbed MRSA. Back then, hardly anyone had heard of it because it hadn't yet hit the headlines.

At the time, some drug users took great quantities of antibiotics in an attempt to stop dirty needles infecting them. The medicine wiped out the junkies' weaker germs, leaving the stronger ones to multiply in their place. Unknowingly, the drug users had developed mutant bacteria with antibiotic-resistant genes within their bodies. Whenever they ended up in hospital, they passed around copies of the resilient genes, turning the resident bugs into untreatable superbugs and creating MRSA.

It was the new MRSA superbug that killed Damian's mother after a simple operation to remove her appendix.

And Damian swore that one day he'd get even.

CHAPTER 7

Damian Brack was in Shaughney's own living room. Twenty-five years old, seventy-five per cent down the road towards Brad Pitt, rugged, fantastically floppy hair, and cute with it. Not bad at all. And yet Shaughney wasn't really in the mood. She felt wounded. But what was in her mum's eyes when she looked at Damian? Admiration, Shaughney thought. What sort of admiration? She hoped it was purely professional and medical.

'So,' Damian was saying to Mollie, 'you think you could have brought it home on your uniform last Thursday night, after tending Bill Garvey.' He glanced at Shaughney and then concentrated on her mum again. 'Did you two come into contact while you were still wearing it?'

'Shaughney pulled me up out of a chair.'

Turning his attention to Shaughney, he asked, 'What did you do straight after?'

She shrugged. 'Not sure. I probably got homework out of my bag.'

'And it was the next day – Friday – you saw this unknown man?'

She nodded. 'Outside school.'

Her mum chipped in. 'How come? What was he doing?'

Shaughney didn't know if she wanted to let on about Finn Pallister. 'He . . . er . . . asked for directions.'

'Did you make any sort of contact with him?'

'No.'

'None at all?'

'No. But . . .'

'What?' Damian prompted.

'I dropped my bag and he picked it up.'

'Mmm. If your bag was contaminated and he got some on his hands, he might've transferred it to his mouth.'

Butting in, Shaughney's mum said, 'We're lucky *we* didn't.'

'Very,' Damian agreed. 'I'll take your bag for tests, Shaughney, but any bacteria on it will be dead by now. They'll only thrive in the warm and wet.'

'All right.'

Mollie asked, 'Doesn't it frighten you to be in the same room with us?'

Damian smiled. 'I think I can handle it.'

'We could be carrying the germ.'

'I don't think you are,' he said. 'If it was still alive and kicking, you'd be pretty ill by now.'

'But you're still taking a gamble.'

'My job puts me in the firing line, yes. But . . .' He shrugged. 'I'm not as reckless as you think. Even if I got infected, I trust Professor Monkhouse to come up with a cure before I peg out. Don't be fooled by her appearance. Some people make a mistake, thinking she's too chic to be clever. But she's more than clever. She's brilliant.'

'She's certainly . . . different. Some people might think she's too distant to care.'

'That's a mistake as well. You don't have to be in everyone's face all the time to prove you're humane. If anyone's going to crack this, Rosalind will. She just needs a bit of space to think.' Damian turned his intense eyes on Shaughney. 'I don't understand about Adam Satchwell. You see him at this Teen and Toddler Scheme, but I thought that was just Mondays.'

'It is,' Shaughney answered. 'But I bumped into him on Friday night as well. I was visiting . . . a friend and I caught him before he fell over.' Suddenly she stopped, her face pale.

'What is it?'

'I've just remembered. He started sucking his thumb straight after I'd touched his hand! It's . . .'

Damian seemed to guess what had struck her so abruptly. 'No, it's not your fault.'

She was horrified. 'It is!'

'No,' Damian said firmly. 'Look. Do you feel guilty if

you've got a cold and you go out and pass it around?'

Dejected, Shaughney shrugged. 'A bit. Not a lot. Why?'

'Well, that's worse than what you might've done here. You know when you've got a cold. If you mix with your mates, you know what'll happen. You make a deliberate decision to spread it about. This isn't like that. You didn't have a clue you'd got this germ so no one's going to blame you. If you've passed it around, you didn't do it on purpose.'

'Anyway,' Mollie added, reaching towards her daughter, 'if I hadn't brought it home, you wouldn't have been put in this position. I'm sorry, love.'

Shaughney understood their logic but she still felt devastated. 'But poor little Adam. And who else might I . . . you know?'

'That's one reason I'm here,' Damian replied, switching back from compassionate to businesslike instantly. 'I want you to make a list – I don't care how long it is – of everyone you've come into contact with from last Thursday night. Especially Friday. Names and as many addresses as you can. If you don't know an address, put down a telephone number or whatever.' He gave her a notepad and biro. 'If our second patient was conscious, he could tell me who he is and who his contacts are. I'm already tracing Bill Garvey's visitors and Adam Satchwell's movements. The idea is to build a complete picture. Maybe – just maybe – I can see where this thing came from, where it's going, and who's likely to catch it.'

Before he left, Damian took saliva samples from them both. While Shaughney stood in front of him with her mouth open and eyes closed, he pushed a bud of cotton wool against her inner cheek and rolled it around. Normally, she would have kept her eyes open to watch him during a medical procedure that felt almost intimate, but flirting wasn't top of her priorities any more.

When he'd finished, he explained, 'The lab's got blood samples from you already, but I want to see if there's anything different about the conditions in your mouths. You see, maybe you *were* lucky – simply because you didn't transfer the bug to your mouths or noses – but maybe you weren't. You might've got a good dose but you're both immune. That'd be great news to say the least. Unlikely, but tremendous.'

Showing him to the door, Shaughney's mum asked, 'Assuming we're not immune, though, what's your best advice for stopping it getting a grip?'

With a playful grin, he replied, 'Don't bite your nails or pick your nose.'

CHAPTER 8

The woman on film looked away from the camera for a moment and then took a deep breath. 'After the first infection event,' she reported, 'an almost complete picture was pieced together through exhaustive interviews with survivors and witnesses like Caitlin Satchwell. To assist with the task, a police officer called Inspector O'Connell brought in psychologists who specialise in helping witnesses to remember what they've seen. Usually their techniques are required for recalling a crime scene but, at this point, there was no crime, except in the case of Curtis Bennett. Even so, their methods were invaluable to the medical investigation of the outbreak.

'It's ironic that Angus Kerven spat the harmless *Mycoplasma perrium* onto a pavement where the Satchwells unwittingly carried it into the Royal Liverpool because – once Mr Garvey became the medium for turning it into a fatal superbug and his nurse's uniform became the vehicle for its journey back out into the community – its next two hosts were Angus Kerven and Adam Satchwell. By coincidence, the nurse's daughter – Shaughney Willett – met and apparently unknowingly infected them both.

'They were not the only victims.'

PART 3
ESCALATION

CHAPTER 1

There were compensations in having to crash out of the fire exit on Monday and disappear into the dark corners of Pembroke Place to escape from the terrorist who'd been tracking Finn. It meant Karl avoided the dirty nappies at the Teen and Toddler Scheme and he got another visit from Shaughney. And that wasn't the only result. Karl and Finn found out from Shaughney that the man with the Toyota had become a hospital case.

Uncharitably, Finn muttered, 'Good. One down, two to go.'

'Not very sympathetic,' Shaughney replied, smiling.

She had a nice smile, Karl thought. The smile of a rogue. Despite the giant red earrings and pouty lips, she wasn't glamorous like some sex-symbol actress. She was far grittier than that. Sharp and tough, she looked ready for a scrap.

She fixed her eyes on him and said, 'Have you still got that book they're after?'

Karl nodded. 'Yes.' He'd hidden it in one of his cupboards.

Puzzling Karl, she asked if it mentioned anything about throats and mouths. He hadn't seen anything like that and, once he'd told her, Shaughney left with Grace.

After they'd gone, Karl said to Finn, 'What was that all about?'

'Dunno,' Finn answered. 'But they keep coming round here.'

With a giant grin, Karl puffed out his chest and ran a hand through his hair. 'That's because Shaughney fancies me.' Deep down, he knew it wasn't true. 'And because Grace fancies you.'

'Huh.'

'She must like the boisterous-looking ones.'

'What?'

'That's what they called you in the paper. Boisterous.'

Finn grunted again. 'I'll look it up and get back to you.'

The next few days were manic. All sorts of rumours were flying about. People said that little Adam Satchwell was poorly in hospital. Word on the street was that four other kids and two mums from the Teen and Toddler Scheme had been taken ill. And Karl's room no longer pulsated because the man upstairs who served fish and chips in the neighbourhood take-away had also been admitted to the Royal Liverpool. Everyone was gossiping about a rampant virus, iffy hygiene at the hospital, dodgy throats, hysteria, diseased asylum seekers spreading a foreign sickness around, and a government plot.

The local media couldn't shed any light on it. They managed only to extract a promise from a Professor Rosalind Monkhouse that she would make an announcement when there was something definite to announce.

On Friday, Karl sat in one of Mr Dee's lessons and yawned. He told himself that the outbreak was nothing to do with Eve Perry because her creation couldn't stick to people's insides. It couldn't infect anyone. It said as much in the laboratory book. Besides, her bacteria were safely caged in a university laboratory – in a cabinet that was sealed to her orphaned life form. Even so, something that Mr Dee had said last week and Shaughney's question about mouths and throats niggled at him. And there was the timing. This bout of illness had struck soon after Dr Perry's death. The doubt in his mind would not go away.

For the third time, Mr Dee took a deep breath and held it for a few seconds. Then he blew into a plastic tube. On the bench in front of him, his breath bubbled through cloudy limewater. He held up the jar. 'See? It's milky. That proves when I breathe out, there's a lot of carbon dioxide. Us humans turn oxygen and food – like carbohydrates – into carbon dioxide and water. Plants do the opposite. With the help of sunlight, they turn carbon dioxide and water into oxygen, carbohydrates and other nutrients. It's a beautifully designed arrangement. Plants love our lifestyle. We breathe out their favourite food and our industries chuck billions of tonnes of it into the atmosphere. As a result, we might get faster growing crops – more food – but most scientists think we're ruining the climate at the same time.'

Karl didn't hear the rest of the lesson – more on global warming – because his brain went down a different avenue.

After the lesson, when he approached Mr Dee, the teacher scowled and said, 'You look thoughtful. Apparently, too thoughtful to listen to me half the time.'

'Yeah, well . . . You know Eve Perry? I was thinking about the bacteria she . . . er . . . might've made. The paper said it'd cut climate change by eating up carbon dioxide.'

'Ah, you were listening a bit, then.'

'If that's true, it'd like us because we breathe it out.'

'Yes,' the teacher replied. 'Humans, monkeys, birds, fungi and lots of others – including normal bacteria – take oxygen from the air and put out carbon dioxide. But, from what I read, Dr Perry had the idea of designing a bug that works the other way round – like a plant. She was going to give her bacterium the genes that would make it dine on carbon dioxide.' He hesitated before adding, 'If she'd made it, yes, I suppose it'd be attracted to us because we're a ready-made meal. It'd be particularly fond of our lungs, noses, mouths and throats.'

Karl nodded. 'Thought so.' Steeling himself, he said, 'Didn't you say nasty bugs sometimes pass genes to the harmless ones, turning them bad?'

'You remembered something from last week! I was beginning to think you all forgot my words of wisdom as soon as you walked out the door.' He was trying to keep it light-hearted but there was always an edge in his voice when he came across youthful disrespect.

'But is it right?'

'Spot on. Ten out of ten. Starred A.'

'Thanks, sir.' Karl sauntered out of the science laboratory, not exactly dashing towards Languages.

It was only a short walk along Brownlow Hill to the university. Karl and Finn stopped and consulted a campus map to find which building was the School of Biological Sciences because Karl was eager to take a look at the laboratory where Eve Perry used to work.

Some way behind the boys, a car also came to a halt, but they didn't notice it. The sun had set and the two men in the car avoided parking under a streetlamp.

While Karl squinted at the roadside map, Finn shuffled on the spot, itching to move on. 'I wish you were Bouncer. He can look pretty mean when he wants to. You don't scare people so much.'

'Don't need to be scary tonight. It's not that sort of raid,' Karl assured him.

'But how are we going to get in?'

'I had this plan to walk through the front door.'

'What? It'll be locked up for the night, I bet, and people will see – or hear – if we put a brick through it.'

'Not tonight.'

'Why not?'

Karl smiled. 'I saw some posters. They're holding a public lecture and, if it's a public lecture, it must be open to the public. No problem. We walk in, sneak off, find Eve Perry's lab and check it out.'

'What's this lecture thing, then?'

'Don't panic. We don't have to sit through it. But we might have to say we're going to when we get there. It's something about sex, fertility and reproduction. The pictures might be good. Pity we're going to miss them.'

'And if some big beefy bouncer stops us at the door . . .?'

'We say the school sent us. Our science teacher recommended it to help with biology coursework. Come on,' Karl said. He tapped the layout of the campus. 'I know where it is now.'

It wasn't like a queue at the cinema for the first showing of the latest blockbuster. Even so, there were a few people waiting expectantly outside the university's biology department. They didn't look like Finn and Karl's sort of crowd, but the boys did their best to blend in. And they slid into the building at the same time as a group of university students. Inside, people were standing around in the foyer talking earnestly. None of them seemed to be discussing tomorrow's football, but sex was the main topic of conversation. At least Karl had one fascination that he shared with these brainy types.

Karl made straight for a display of mug shots of the department's teaching staff. Underneath each photograph was a name and room number. 'Makes it easy,' he said quietly to Finn. He pointed out the picture of Eve Perry, not yet removed from the showcase. In the photo, her closed mouth was a thin straight line. Too serious to form a smile, she looked exactly the same as she had done in the local newspaper. Her expression was very different from the grotesque and bloody face that had confronted Karl and Finn in Brownlow Hill. 'Room 515,' Karl muttered. 'Bet it's on the fifth floor.'

On the left of the entrance there were toilets, a lift and a corridor. If the boys called for the lift, someone was bound to query what they were doing and where they were going because the door to the main lecture room was in the foyer, on the right-hand side. There was no reason to take the lift. Instead, the boys sidled towards the toilets and then slipped quickly through the swing doors into the corridor that channelled through one arm of the building like an artery.

No one followed them or shouted or set off an alarm,

so they tiptoed down the long passageway that was dimly lit, empty and quiet, like a school corridor after hours. There were doors to offices and small laboratories on either side and all of them had numbers that began with zero. At the end, just before a fire door to the outside world, there was a narrow set of stone steps on the right. The boys looked at each other and then began to climb the stairs noiselessly.

Counting the flights, they emerged through some swing doors on the fifth floor. The passageway that stretched in front of them was as eerily still as the one below. Here, the numbers on the doors began with 5, so they crept along until they arrived at Room 515. The nameplate had been unscrewed and removed, and the door was protected by a combination lock.

Finn let out an audible groan. 'Now what?'

'Er . . . Let's try—'

Finn interrupted. 'Yeah. All the numbers from zero to nine-nine-nine-nine. It'll only take a day and a half.'

'Shush. I'm thinking. Got it!' When Karl punched 1-1-3-2 on the keypad, the lock clicked open.

Finn was wide-eyed. 'How did you do that?' he exclaimed in a whisper.

'Magic,' Karl replied with a grin as he pushed the door open a little. 'Or remembering the number Eve Perry wrote at the beginning of her lab book.' He peered inside but could see nothing in the unlit room. At least the darkness meant there was no one within.

The boys took a final look up and down the corridor, then edged inside. Finn extracted a torch from his coat pocket and turned it on. Sweeping the beam across the room, Finn picked out a corner cubicle that had provided Dr Perry with some office space, a couple of benches stacked with scientific equipment, dishes and bottles, a deep freeze, an incubator, and another door. The inner door was inscribed with big red letters: *BIOHAZARD. Authorised personnel only.* He brought the spotlight to a halt on the ominous warning.

Karl nodded. 'That'll be what we want.'

Finn shrugged. 'I still don't know what we're doing here.'

'Neither do I,' Karl replied in a hushed voice. 'Not really. I just think there's got to be something that'll make sense of it all.'

'Oh yeah?'

Solemnly, they both walked towards the internal door. It felt as if they were defiling a pharaoh's tomb. And, if films were anything to go by, explorers who did that were usually cursed.

CHAPTER 2

The door to the inner crypt would not open. It had a conventional lock and there was no sign of the key. Finn looked as if he didn't want to find it. 'Biohazard. Isn't that dangerous?' he asked.

Karl was not to be turned aside now. 'Nah. I just want to take a look inside, not touch anything.' He looked around, then said, 'The boxed-in bit. That'll be where she'd keep the key.' He led the way to the *en suite* office in the corner.

The area was about the same size as a bathroom. Instead of a toilet and bath there was a grey filing cabinet and a big desk with two computers perched on top. Attached to the wall were shelves, heavy with books and science magazines. On top of the books was a collection of soft toys: a black hairy spider, a curved purple sailfish, a cute octopus with its furry tentacles dangling over the book spines, a fluffy kitten and quite a few more.

Finn nudged Karl and whispered, 'She liked her animals.'

Trying not to get distracted, Karl opened the

drawers of Dr Perry's desk one at a time and rummaged around inside while Finn held the spotlight. They were cluttered and messy as if someone else had already disturbed them. Maybe it was just that Dr Perry was untidy. By the time Karl had been through the contents of all but one drawer, he was wondering if he was barking up the wrong tree. His mood altered, though, when he delved into the bottom left-hand drawer and found a bunch of three keys. The largest one looked hopeful.

On the way back to the locked door, both Karl and Finn stopped dead at the same time. There were footsteps and voices outside in the corridor. Instinctively, the boys ducked down behind one of the benches and Finn turned off his torch. Hearts in their mouths, they waited without saying a word.

But the footsteps receded and the voices trailed away.

'Phew!' Finn breathed, turning the torch back on again. It picked out an ominous white overall that looked like a space suit hanging on the wall on their right.

Standing up again, they returned to the door with the biohazard warning sign. The big key fitted the lock and turned easily. As soon as Karl let go of the key and reached for the handle, Finn grabbed his arm. 'Are you sure?' he checked.

'Certain.'

Finn let out a long breath and nodded. 'Okay. Let's do it.'

It was a windowless room, larger than the boys had expected. Against the wall were three vast airtight units made of sturdy panes of glass with massive vents on top. Each fume cupboard had two armholes with sealed-in rubber gloves so that Dr Perry could work on anything inside without coming into skin contact with it or breathing the air surrounding it. Underneath the fume cupboards, there were lockers with their doors wide open as if someone in a hurry had peered inside. But it was the bench behind the door that caught Karl's eye. 'Look,' he said quietly, pointing.

Sitting on the tabletop was a cabinet. The glass at the front had been marked with a black felt-tip pen: *Mycoplasma pe* . . . The rest was missing because the glass had been shattered. On the floor underneath, fragments of glass twinkled like stars in Finn's torchlight. Behind the broken pane of the box was a row of small dishes.

'I think that's what we don't touch,' Karl muttered.

'How did it end up like that?' Finn said.

'An accident or . . .'

'What?'

'Sabotage, I suppose. Either way, whatever was inside got out. And I reckon it was Perry's homemade bug.'

Finn shrugged. 'Yeah?'

To make sure his friend realised what he was saying, Karl added, 'That means Frankenstein's creature's on the loose.'

'Just as well it can't kill anyone – that's what you said. And there's a medicine for it.'

Karl suppressed a cough and went back into the main part of the laboratory, pausing to lock the biohazard room again. 'But it might've turned into a germ that's going round attacking people ... Come on. We've got to find Notebook 7A. That's where she put stuff about the antidote.' Still carrying the bunch of keys, he headed back for the office part. 'If we grab it, we can be heroes in all this. We go to the hospital and say, "It's in here. Everything you want to know about a medicine. Just give it to everyone and panic over." Just like that.'

Karl was certain that Shaughney also suspected a link between Dr Perry, the new life form, carbon dioxide and the respiratory tract infections sweeping the area. She wouldn't have asked about throats and mouths if she weren't making the same connection. In planning to bring an end to the outbreak, Karl was also thinking of impressing Shaughney.

Feeling excited and nervy in equal measure, Karl pointed at the bookshelves and said, 'Up there.'

Obliging him, Finn ran the spotlight along the spines, picking out titles and soppy toys. Mostly, the volumes were printed books and magazines. There was nothing that looked similar to the lab notebook Eve had already given them. When the beam reached the end of the shelving, completing a fruitless search, Karl sighed.

'There's always that,' Finn said softly, shining the light on the filing cabinet.

Karl nodded. 'Good idea.' He pulled on the first of four drawers but it refused to budge. He imagined that the lock at the top right of the unit was engaged. Glancing down at the three keys in his hand, Karl smiled. Taking the smallest key in his fingers, he pushed it into the lock and turned. The catch disengaged with a dull clunk.

Getting itchy, Finn whispered, 'Hurry up. We've been here too long already.'

The top drawer opened with a metallic squeal.

'Shush!'

'All right,' Karl replied, more determined than ever. 'I can't help it. Give me some more light in here.'

There was a jumble of papers and folders but nothing resembling a notebook. Again, it looked as if a hurricane had swept through the filing cabinet. Eve Perry had to be the world's most untidy person. Her office was even more messy than Karl's bedroom.

The second drawer made Karl gasp. It contained a series of tatty brown paperback notebooks. Probably they were supposed to sit in order in the hanging files, spines up so their reference numbers could be read at a glance, but they were chaotic. Some were upside down, some on their sides, in no particular order. 'Bet it's here,' Karl said quietly as he pulled them out one by one, looking for number 7A.

He was about halfway through them when he clutched one of the books and said, 'Got it!' There was a sticky label on the spine that read *Notebook 7A*, and Dr Perry had marked the inside front cover with *7A* in black felt-tip.

'Let's get going, then,' Finn urged.

Karl threw the bunch of keys back into the bottom drawer of the desk and made for the door that led to the corridor.

Finn turned the torch off while Karl opened the door a crack and peeked into the passageway that now looked bright in comparison with the dark laboratory. There was no one around so the boys sneaked out and retraced their steps. Before they got to the stairway, Karl slipped the notebook possessively inside his coat and kept it there by clamping it against his ribs with his left arm.

Their footfalls on the stone steps echoed in the empty stairwell, making them nervous. They feared that someone would hear and investigate the strangers creeping around the School of Biological Sciences. There were a few people in the third-storey corridor but they were some distance from the stairs so Karl and Finn simply quickened their pace. Back on the ground floor, they waited for a woman walking down the passageway to enter one of the rooms and then they strode down the home straight, making for the foyer.

They came to an immediate halt when the middle-aged woman re-emerged from a side-room right in front of them.

She let out a little cry of surprise, then said, 'What are you doing here?'

'Er . . . We were in the lecture – our school sent us – but we had to come out for the loo,' Karl replied, trying to appear calm and innocent. 'Someone told us it was here somewhere but . . .' He shrugged.

Plainly, the woman remained suspicious but she wasn't going to call the cops. 'You came straight past the Gents.' Pointing down the corridor, she said, 'Through the double doors and they're on your left. I don't know how you missed them.'

'Sorry,' Karl said.

'Yeah,' Finn added.

'Um. I'll watch. Make sure you don't miss them again.' With mistrust in her eyes, she glanced at Karl's immobile left arm, held tight to his body.

'Thanks.'

Finn and Karl retreated in silence, pushed past the door and dived into the toilet. Finn leaned on a wall while Karl propped himself against one of the sinks and let out a sigh of relief. 'Phew!'

Finn congratulated him. 'Quick thinking. I would've just kicked her shin and run for it.'

'Bet she's still watching. We'll go out in a minute.' He adjusted Dr Perry's notebook under his coat, ready for their escape.

When they went back into the foyer, they saw the woman standing attentively by the double doors. Karl nodded his thanks towards her before shooting out of the building with Finn.

Outside in the drizzle, Finn muttered, 'Made it! No trouble.'

But he was wrong. Trouble followed them slyly back to the flats.

CHAPTER 3

Finn Pallister was too young to be on the Electoral Roll so Smith and Bennett could not discover his address like that. There were few Pallisters in the phone book, and none in the right area of Liverpool. Another dead end. And Kingsway School refused to reveal any information on one of its pupils. Smith and Bennett weren't even sure if it was Pallister who had Dr Perry's lab book. It could have been his pal and they had no idea who he was.

'Are you sure his name was Pallister? Is that definitely what Angry said?' Curtis Bennett asked, frustrated at their lack of progress.

'Yes,' Smith answered, his voice sounding even deeper and more gruff than usual.

'Pity we can't check. If we went to see him in hospital, they'd ask us some awkward questions.'

'The police'll identify Kerven before long. He's got a criminal record – breaking and entering on a nuclear waste job – so they'll match him with the right file sooner or later.'

'It's down to you and me now.'

'Yeah,' Smith replied. 'We'll have to hang around Kingsway School or that block of flats till we see Pallister and his mate.' He put his hand over his mouth and coughed. Afterwards, he probed the roof of his mouth with his tongue. It felt different, more ridged than normal.

Bennett nodded. 'We tail them till we find out exactly where they live. Then, next time they go out, we turn their places over.'

Weston Smith shook his head. 'Won't work.'

'Why not?' Bennett responded impatiently.

'It'd be all right if they lived in houses but they don't. It's a block of flats. We might get away with it if they both live on the ground floor – watching which ones they go into – but if they go upstairs we can't follow them without making it obvious what we're doing. If we lag far enough behind so they don't cotton on, we wouldn't see which flats they go into. They've already proved they're crafty sods, good at giving us the slip.'

'Okay. So what's the solution?'

'The simple direct approach. We confront them, tackle them head-on.'

Damian interrupted his work when Shaughney Willett turned up at the Royal Liverpool after school on Friday, asking to speak to him. Intrigued, he took her to a small conference room. 'What can I do for you?' he said with a friendly smile. Then, concerned that she might be

121

about to tell him she was ill, he frowned and added, 'Are you feeling all right?'

'I'm fine.'

'That's good. You should be, because your blood was negative. You can have your schoolbag back as well. It's clean. We're still testing your saliva sample. Nothing to report yet.'

'This isn't about me.'

'Oh? What, then?'

She was fidgeting with one of her earrings. The red hoop was big enough to make a perch for a small bird. 'When I gave you that list of people I'd met, I should've said a bit more about a couple of the boys.'

Damian interrupted. 'Oh? Which ones?'

'Karl Stephenson and Finn Pallister. They might know what's going on.'

'How do you mean?'

'Well, you know the woman at the university who was trying to make life from scratch?'

'Yes. Dr Perry. Rosalind was interviewed about it on the news.' He reached out and gently touched Shaughney's arm. 'Go on. You were going to say about these boys.'

'Let me ask you something first. This germ, it attacks the nose and mouth, doesn't it?'

Damian nodded. 'Our first patient – Mr Garvey – has died from respiratory or heart failure, I'm afraid. It targeted his whole respiratory system. Adam Satchwell and the man you found are going the same way.'

Her face creased with concern – probably for the toddler – but she seemed determined to keep to her important message. 'Well, the thing that Dr Perry made was designed to live on carbon dioxide so it'd like human breath, wouldn't it?'

'*If* she made it and if it ever came into contact with human breath, yes, I suppose so.' Still wearing his smile, Damian said, 'I'm beginning to see where you're going, but it'd be confined to the lab.'

'Maybe it isn't,' Shaughney replied. 'Karl and Finn said there was something funny going on. They were there when Dr Perry died and so was that guy with the bloody mouth. He was chasing her when she gave Karl some notes on her experiments . . .'

'Hang on, Shaughney,' Damian said, suffering from overload. 'Slow down. This could be crucial. I've got to ask you some questions, but . . .' He decided that Rosalind should eavesdrop on their conversation. He pointed to the TV screen and said, 'I'm going to turn this video-conferencing system on so Professor Monkhouse can join us from her hotel. All right? It's important she hears what you've got to say.'

Shaughney looked disappointed by the intrusion but she nodded anyway.

While he made the link to Rosalind, he said, 'After you've told us the whole story, I think you're going to have to take me to see this Karl and Finn.'

*

Heading for home through the dismal evening, Finn said to Karl, 'PlayStation, is it, when we get back?' But he hesitated before adding, 'Oh. No. I'll have to walk Bouncer first.'

Whilst Finn's mind had moved on to the mundane, Karl's still seemed to be chewing over their raid on the university. 'You know, if someone else broke in and smashed that cabinet, it doesn't add up.'

Finn wasn't that bothered but he replied, 'Why's that?' Then he blew a raindrop from his nose.

'Well, did you see any doors or locks that'd been forced?'

Finn shrugged. 'No. It just means they did the same as us.'

'Yeah. That's why the drawers were in such a mess. But how did they know the combination for the lock?'

Finn opened the door to the block of flats and said, 'Don't ask me.'

'If Eve Perry was inside when they went in, maybe it wouldn't have been locked.'

'That type locks every time the door shuts. Like the ones at school. If you haven't got the code, you can only open them from the inside.'

'Yeah. You're right. And they couldn't have ransacked the place if she was there. She could've disturbed *them*, though. She would've guessed they were after her lab book so she grabbed it and made a run for it. They chased her and . . .'

'She got splattered in the road, trying to get away.'

Karl nodded. 'Exactly. They might've gone back that night to see if there was anything else they wanted to nick. But I still don't know how they got in without clobbering the door in the first place.'

'They'd got the code.'

'Yeah.' Karl hesitated by the stairwell. Tapping his side where the second notebook nestled within his coat, he said, 'I'm going up to put this somewhere safe.'

'I'll come up to yours after I've seen to Bouncer. Okay?'

'Sure.' Karl turned and leapt up the stairs two at a time.

'Great night to walk the dog,' Finn muttered sarcastically to himself as he trudged along the passageway on autopilot, blind to the permanent graffiti.

As usual, there was no one at home apart from Bouncer. Finn was filling up his water bowl when the beginnings of a growl formed in the dog's throat. Finn looked round at his restless and suddenly alert pet. 'What's—?'

He didn't get to the end of the sentence before the door crashed inwards and two men barged through it. Finn recognised them at once. The dog bowl slipped from his fingers and crashed into the sink.

CHAPTER 4

Standing in front of Finn, Bouncer bared his teeth and let out a fearsome snarl followed by a loud bark.

One of the intruders – the wiry one – came to an immediate stop, trembling at the sight of the Alsatian, but the shorter muscular guy came forward boldly, holding Bouncer's gaze. He put out his hand and said, 'Hiya there, boy. You're a good dog, aren't you? All bark and no bite.'

Just when Finn needed Bouncer to be as ferocious as his appearance, the daft dog let the side down by accepting a pat on the head from the stranger. Worse, he moved to nestle against the terrorist's leg.

The man grinned at Finn. 'Always had a way with dogs,' he said in a croaky voice. His smile was insincere and he held his mouth oddly open as if he'd just bitten on something that tasted disgusting.

Finn's mouth was open as well, but he didn't say anything. He just stared at the intruders.

'I guess you're wondering why we want words with you,' said the man who was stroking Bouncer.

Finn swallowed nervously. Actually, he was

wondering how he was going to escape. He didn't think he'd got much of a chance in a fight or a mad scramble for the door, but he didn't know any other way.

'Don't worry. We're not going to—'

Interrupting him, Finn blurted out, 'You're terrorists!'

The stocky chap's eyes opened wide. 'Terrorists!' He threw back his head and laughed. 'Is that what you think we are?'

Behind him, the other one managed only a twisted grin.

'Yes.'

'Wrong. We're campaigners. Environmental activists, not terrorists. The press call us Green Warriors. That's not terror, that's caring about people and the environment.'

Finn was recovering slowly from the shock of the break-in and his brain had engaged again. 'That's what a terrorist *would* say. And smashing your way into my place . . . That's what terrorists would do.'

'Look. You know about Eve Perry. You've got her write-up. I know it's complicated, but you must've worked out what she's done. She's the terrorist. Not us. She's put everyone at risk by making an unnatural and dangerous organism.'

Finn was more concerned with the breaking and entering. 'What are you going to do to me?'

'Nothing. Not if you hand over that notebook she

gave you. We take it and leave. That's it. You won't see us again.'

'Yeah. So you can make some sort of bomb.'

'No! That's exactly what we're trying to stop. Don't you see? Without those notes, no one else can repeat what she's done. No one'll turn it into a weapon.'

'I don't trust you. Why should I? Why should I believe someone who's just barged in?'

Behind the two men, Karl appeared in the doorway with both the blue and brown laboratory books in his hands. 'Before you take Bouncer for—' He stopped dead when he saw what was happening.

'Ah,' the rough bloke said, flashing another smile. 'Spot on. Excellent timing. Come and join the party. Looks like you've brought what we want.'

Karl took a step backwards, but did not run away.

Finn guessed that his friend wouldn't leave him at the mercy of thugs. He shouted, 'They say they're not terrorists. They're green activists, whatever that means.'

'It means we want to put a complete stop to Eve Perry's work. To do that, we need her notes.' He held out a hand towards Karl.

'No!' Karl cried, wrapping his arms protectively around the pads. 'I don't believe you.'

'How can I prove it?' the man replied.

'Perry was working on a way of beating global warming. Real greens would like that.'

He shook his head. 'Fewer cars, more insulation and alternative fuels are the answer. A lot less risky than making a new species. That's just adding to the danger. It's more pollution when you think about it. Out of the frying pan into the fire.'

Karl glanced at Finn but neither of them said a word.

'All right,' the burly activist said. 'What would a terrorist do with Perry's notes?'

'Study them. Turn her bug into a biological weapon.'

'Exactly. We want to shred the lot or burn them, destroy every last trace. That's the green thing to do. That's the way to stop it being used in germ warfare.'

Karl hesitated for a few seconds, then opened the blue lab notebook. He took hold of several pages in his fist and said, 'So, you won't mind me ripping these pages to bits.'

'Go ahead. Be my guest,' the unwelcome visitor replied.

Finn and Karl both eyed him suspiciously. If this man was bluffing, he was very good at it. The taller one gave the game away, though. He was failing in his attempt to appear indifferent. He looked horrified at the thought of the book's destruction.

Finn knew that Karl was bluffing as well. His mate was planning to take both notebooks to the hospital. That was Karl's idea for ending the outbreak. Now, in Finn's own front room, it was like one of those face-offs in films and games. The actors were pointing guns at each other's heads with their fingers hooked around the triggers. Who would squeeze first?

Breaking the deadlock, the taller activist made his move. Amazing all of them, he turned swiftly and landed a heavy punch on his colleague's cheek. Droplets of blood flew from his open mouth as he fell over Bouncer and hit the carpet with a heavy thud. The other intruder snatched the blue book from a stunned Karl. Wasting no time, he pushed his way past Karl towards the door.

Bouncer backed away and began to bark again but showed no sign of bravery or interest in a chase. Instead, he licked the injured environmental campaigner's face.

In the doorway, the man with the lab book securely in his hand crashed into Shaughney Willett and someone who was with her. Shaughney let out a cry, midway between a scream and a curse. The thief didn't hesitate. He shouldered the visitors out of his way and made a run for it.

Coming to his senses, Karl thrust Notebook 7A at Shaughney and cried, 'That's important!' Then he took off in pursuit.

Finn followed his friend's example, bursting into a sprint.

Damian looked at the man on the floor and at once recognised the symptoms: the open mouth, the dreadful wheezing and trickle of blood. As a medic first and foremost, he couldn't leave someone who needed his help. He couldn't be distracted by whatever was going on. He dropped to his knees, took a closer look and then called the emergency number on his mobile.

Behind him, Shaughney was bewildered. She was in Finn's apartment, with no Finn, holding some sort of jotter, staring at a cowardly Alsatian and another victim of the insatiable microbe.

CHAPTER 5

Curtis Bennett didn't really have a choice. That green fool Smith would have happily remained in Pallister's flat and witnessed the destruction of Eve Perry's historic record. Curtis could not allow it to be lost to science for ever. He could not stand by while a mere schoolboy ripped such a valuable and unique document to pieces. He had to save the lab book and escape with it. But the car waiting outside belonged to Weston Smith and the keys were in Smith's pocket. Ignoring the parked car, Curtis sped straight past it with those two boys at his heels.

Clutching the precious notebook in one hand, he raced past the Catholic cathedral and dodged through some of the university campus to cut off a corner.

Behind him, one of the brats shouted, 'Stop him! He's nicked something.'

It was getting late and there weren't many people about. No one who heard made a move or tried to tackle him. They probably assumed that it was the two teenagers who were up to no good.

Pushing past a couple of students, Curtis charged between the sports centre and the Department of Architecture, making for Abercromby Square. He knew that there were always taxis buzzing around there. Every morning, they delivered people to the university. At this time in the evening, they'd be whisking visitors away from the area. If he hadn't shaken off the stupid boys by the time he got to the square, he'd power away from them in a cab. Judging by their shabby flats and cheap clothing, they would not have the cash to pay for a cab to follow him. They'd probably never taken a taxi ride in their lives. Buses and legs were more like it for their sort.

Curtis smirked as he raised his other arm to hail a black cab.

Chests heaving, Karl and Finn ground to a halt at the same time. On the pavement outside the Faculty of Social and Environmental Studies, they watched the taxi take off at speed down Oxford Street towards Mount Pleasant. And both of them let out a tired groan. 'Bugger!' Karl muttered angrily. In a way, it was like the moment two weeks ago when they waved goodbye to the two men trapped on a train. This time, moods were reversed. It was Karl and Finn who were left feeling deflated.

Neither of them believed for a single moment that the third man – the one in the cab – was a green activist,

133

intent on destroying the laboratory notes. The boys didn't know what he was, but they believed that they'd let Dr Perry down. When the cab disappeared from view, they turned round and began to trudge back to Finn's apartment.

There was an ambulance outside and the motionless activist was being taken away. Welcoming Finn home, Bouncer put his front paws on Finn's chest and licked his face. Shaughney was still inside, looking at the brown lab book with the man she'd brought to the flats.

'Are you some sort of cop?' Karl asked, eyeing him suspiciously. He looked too young, though.

'Nothing like,' he replied. 'I'm some sort of doctor. A germ hunter, if you like. Damian Brack. I'm stationed at the hospital.' He jerked his head in its direction.

Karl glanced at Shaughney and she nodded her approval.

'All right,' Karl said. 'We've got some talking to do.'

Damian smiled. 'You're not kidding. What was that all about? And what's this?' He pointed at Notebook 7A.

'We lost the most important one, but that's got a cure for your germ.'

'What?' he exclaimed.

Karl and Finn nodded.

'How do you . . .? Never mind. It'll wait. I want to introduce you to my boss, but there's something to do up at the hospital first. Grab yourselves a spare set of clothes and let's get going.'

In a sterile room at the Royal Liverpool, Damian examined the boys and took blood samples before putting them – and himself – through a scorching ten-minute power-shower with antiseptic soap. He also insisted on a complete change of clothes before escorting them down the hill to meet Professor Rosalind Monkhouse. And a police officer called O'Connell who'd been brought in to hear the boys' story and to quiz them on everything they'd seen, heard, touched and done.

As soon as Karl entered the professor's suite of rooms at the hotel, he found himself looking at a woman he recognised. 'I saw you . . . You're famous! You were on the telly.'

Rosalind waved him towards a seat and said with a pained smile, 'Hmm. I reassured the nation that Dr Perry would have any new life form under tight control. You've come to tell me different, I think.'

Karl liked her. She was putting on a bit too much weight around her middle, he noticed, but it was really her attitude that appealed to him. She might be famous but she wasn't talking down to him. She seemed to be treating him as an equal. Encouraged, Karl opened up and told her all the incredible things that had happened to them since Eve Perry's accident. It felt like far more than two weeks' worth of action. Karl's description was interspersed with the occasional, 'Yeah,' from Finn and queries from the attentive biologist.

'So,' Rosalind said without a hint of accusation in her voice, 'you broke into her lab at the university?'

Karl had anticipated the question so he'd had time to figure out an answer. 'Not really, because Dr Perry gave us the combination.'

'When? How?'

'It was in the book she gave us – a bit like giving us a key – so she mustn't have minded us going in.'

'Tell me again what you saw.'

And so it went on. No one noticed how late it was getting until Inspector O'Connell offered to call Karl's and Finn's parents to reassure them that their children were safe and not in trouble with the law.

When Rosalind allowed the police officer to hijack the conversation, he seemed far more interested in learning from Karl and Finn rather than trying to trick them or arrest them for anything. That didn't mean they trusted him, but he was the first policeman they'd met who conducted a friendly interrogation and operated a laptop while he talked.

At one point, O'Connell interrupted his flow of questions. Scrutinising his monitor, he said to Rosalind, 'It looks like I've just got an identity for your unknown patient – the first extremist. A sharp-eyed copper's spotted it and emailed. Angus Kerven. He's got a record for breaking and entering a harbour site when a ship carrying spent nuclear fuel for reprocessing was coming in.' He turned the laptop round and showed them the on-screen picture. 'Is that him?'

Karl, Finn and Damian all nodded at the same time. 'Yes.'

'Right. I'll give you a printout of everything we know about him. He's got a string of minor offences, all to do with direct action on pollution.' He glanced at Karl and added, 'That probably makes him a genuine Green Warrior, not a bioterrorist.'

'Ah.'

He looked towards Rosalind again. 'What's his condition?'

'He's undergone surgery and we're waiting. It's too early to say. The first patient was too old – and his infection too advanced – to recover from an operation, so we didn't attempt it. The third's too young and weak. Kerven was a better bet. We cut the infection out and he's got a remote chance. But it's only remote because there's not a single antibiotic that works – a trick the germ learnt from MRSA, no doubt. It'll make a comeback, especially if it's in his lungs. A few other patients are going through the same surgery.' She shook her head to show that she feared the worst.

Inspector O'Connell nodded, looked back at his computer screen, and then turned to the boys. 'My team's checked who owns every car parked near your house –

I mean, flat. One belongs to a different activist: Weston Smith. Do you recognise him?'

It was the familiar face of the thickset guy. 'Yes.'

'Okay. No convictions this time but he's another green. We've got him on video at numerous demonstrations, and his car's never far away from any protest on toxic waste. But your third man . . .' He shrugged. 'Watch this series of mug shots. They're all known associates of Smith and Kerven.' He leaned over the upright screen and pressed the return key.

The slide show didn't last long and it didn't include the man who'd thumped Weston Smith and run away with the lab book.

Trying to be helpful – and showing off – Karl said, 'One of them must've known the university and the biological science bit for sure.'

'Oh?'

'Because they got in Dr Perry's place without smashing the door.'

'Good point. But I need more to go on. Like where that taxi went.'

'Easy,' Karl replied, looking even more pleased with himself. 'It was YS52 WKS. You can trace it and ask the driver.'

The police officer was surprised by Karl's initiative and memory. 'You're sure?'

'Certain. It's an easy one to remember. Almost textspeak for "a year is fifty-two weeks". No problem.'

'Right. Thanks. I'm onto it.' At once, O'Connell started tapping away madly at the keypad.

Rosalind had been listening to the conversation and reading Notebook 7A at the same time until she let out a cry of surprise and excitement. Looking at her assistant and beaming broadly, she jabbed a finger at a complicated chemical structure sketched on one of the later pages. 'Get the chemists on to this straightaway, Damian. Dr Perry calls it Anti-MP – short for Anti-*Mycoplasma perrium*. You see, she gave her bacterium a weak spot, just in case. She incorporated a death gene. Clever woman.' Rosalind could not contain her glee – and her relief. 'She says this Anti-MP drug activates it and blocks the bug's metabolism. Brilliant. No metabolism, no life. It's the perfect answer. If the chemists can't find a sample in her lab, I want them to make bucketfuls of it. The experimental details are in here. Either way, test it on the patients who are about to die. We don't have time for animal experiments, working out best doses, and proper safety procedures. Just do it.'

Damian grabbed the brown notebook and at once made for the door.

Facing Karl and Finn, Rosalind said, 'I really can't thank you two enough. You should be given the freedom of the city. Minimum. It would've been better if we'd got the original write-up as well but you worked out what's going on and you've given us the cure.

Can't ask for much more than that.' With a warm and joyful grin, she added, 'I should offer you both a job.'

Finn muttered, 'I don't want to work on . . .' He shut up when he realised from Karl's expression that the professor was joking.

CHAPTER 6

As the video commentary progressed, the woman's face grew more and more tired against an unchanging and unclear background. It was difficult to pick out what was in shot behind her because it was so fuzzy, but she was certainly indoors. The impression was that she was in a tight space, probably a small room of some sort. Like a crypt.

'Once we found that antibiotics had as much effect on the infection as water on a duck's back – we were in the pits of despair. *Mycoplasma perrium* had stolen the genes for antibiotic-resistance from MRSA. Conventional treatment was impossible. However, late on the night of the eleventh of March, there was an understandable surge of optimism. We discovered – courtesy of two local lads – that Eve Perry had incorporated a death gene into *Mycoplasma perrium*, should anything go wrong. She'd produced a drug – Anti-MP – that would trigger the gene and eradicate her bug. Ideal pest control.

'We administered the drug to the worst cases and the patients' conditions improved almost immediately. Little Adam Satchwell recovered completely. Angus Kerven, Weston Smith, the man who served Shaughney Willett fish and chips, and one of the Teen and Toddler mothers did not pull through, but the rest of the patients survived. With the advent of Anti-MP, the epidemic was averted before it got a real stranglehold.

'It was tempting at this stage to conclude that nature is the world's worst bioterrorist. It allows harmless bacteria to acquire malevolent genes and behaviour, turning them into a hardy killer, leaving a trail of illness and death. There would've been a dire epidemic if it hadn't been for a dedicated medical team, a couple of kids, and the death gene. But that wasn't the end of the affair. We didn't know then that human beings, blessed – or cursed – with greed, ingenuity and brutality, were about to surpass the cruelty of nature.'

PART 4
TERROR

CHAPTER 1

The empty warehouse had the eerie atmosphere of an old abandoned church and Curtis Bennett felt like a sinner. Standing there, waiting for judgement, his every movement on the rough concrete floor echoed around the disused building. Outside, rain pattered on the roof and the gentle waves of the Mersey lapped against the quayside. A rusting dockland crane reached upwards like a cross.

Curtis had first contacted the Fundamentalist Revolutionary Church when, riddled with debt, he was made redundant as a scientist. Knowing about Eve Perry's controversial work and the Green Warriors opposition to it, and having come across a website on the aims of the FRC cult, he saw a way out of his financial predicament. He infiltrated the greens to secure their professional help in getting close to Dr Perry's work. He told them about the working practices of scientists and stood by as Kerven used his charms on a university technician to extract from her the combinations to locks in the School of Biological Sciences.

The Green Warriors always intended to destroy the

experimental details of Eve Perry's work, but *his* ambitions were entirely different. Curtis planned to solve his problems by preserving her secrets and selling them to the Fundamentalist Revolutionary Church for a colossal sum of money. Then he would leave the country and make a fresh start well away from Britain.

Now, the FRC's scientist sat cross-legged on the grimy concrete floor and took his time to inspect the laboratory notebook. He read earnestly, like a zealot studying holy scriptures. The cult's minders were lingering all over the place in case of trouble, like cops on surveillance duty. Five were inside. One held a briefcase and Curtis assumed it contained the money that was due to him. The other four were watching uneasily as the deal took place. Occasionally, they shuffled around, clearly on edge. Curtis suspected that they were carrying weapons under their raincoats. Some more FRC heavies were on guard outside. Curtis tried to remain calm.

The woman he knew only as Ruth walked right around him, speaking in a whisper. She was not ashamed of her words and her views. She spoke softly because her utterances were powerful enough without volume. She believed that what she said was so important that people – and the world – would hush to listen.

'You should join us, Curtis Bennett. You believe in positive action. You could find a home with the Fundamentalist Revolutionary Church. Don't tell me

146

all you want is the money. Surely you've not fallen into the trap of greed for material goods and wealth. It's a sin – and one of the signs that man's time on Earth is nearing its end. You only have to look around. What do you see? I don't mean a disused dock, though this is part of the desecration of God's land. I mean abuse of children and women, the break-up of the family, yobbish behaviour, illicit drugs, crime, underage sex, abortion, lack of respect, homosexuality, the empty adoration of celebrity. Need I go on? I don't think so. I think you can see that this society no longer deserves its place on God's Earth.'

'I ... er ... know what you mean but ...' Curtis shook his head nervously. 'No, it's not for me.'

Further down the river, the Woodside Ferry sounded its strident horn, making Curtis jump. A trickle of water fell from the fractured roof and splashed down a metre to the left of him. Under his breath, he muttered a curse at the wet weather.

Ruth wagged her finger at him. 'Don't complain. Rain is God's gift, sustaining all life. It's liquid sunshine.' She smiled briefly at her own description. Dressed smartly but certainly not in fashionable designer gear, she was approaching sixty and she looked wearied by the modern world. 'The human species has become a plague on the planet. We believe that the time has come for a different sort of plague. Ordained by God, this one will cleanse the world of its most troublesome inhabitants.' She looked up towards the drumming rain. 'Like a great flood washing away everything in its path.'

The man hunched over the laboratory notebook looked up at her and announced, 'There's a problem, Ruth. The bacterium's got a built-in suicide mechanism.'

'Does that make it useless as an instrument of retribution?'

'No,' he answered. 'It's still a superb organism, but she's enfeebled it with a death gene. I'd have to remove that before making a whole lot. With these details,' he said, raising the book slightly, 'I can do that. And I can use her methods to add a couple more genes: one that'll allow it to attach to human cells and another that'll make it release toxins to improve its killing capacity. Then we'd have a real wolf in sheep's clothing.'

'But . . .?'

'I need the drug designed to turn the death gene on. Otherwise, it'd be tricky – maybe impossible – to be sure I've removed it successfully and totally. If I made a batch and the drug had no effect on it, I'd know for certain we've got what we need: a lethal infection without a cure. Obviously, a germ that can be destroyed at a stroke can't be God's instrument of retribution. So, I need that compound. Its formula's in Notebook 7A, according to this.'

'Thank you, James.' Still not raising her voice, Ruth

turned to Curtis. 'What have you got to say about this?'

'I didn't know . . .' Curtis shook his head in frustration. In his mind's eye, he could see Pallister's mate clutching a brown pad with *Notebook 7A* on its spine. But he didn't know the boy's name so he said, 'A boy called Finn Pallister's got it.'

The cross-legged scientist looked up at him. 'Finn Pallister?'

'Yes. Why?'

James shrugged. 'Just checking. An unusual name, that's all.'

Ruth continued to walk around Curtis till she stopped right in front of him. 'You'll have to get it off him and bring it to us.'

Curtis frowned. 'That wasn't part of the deal. I've delivered what you asked for. Besides, Pallister knows me now. It'd be too dangerous for me because he'd spot me coming.'

Ruth was quiet for a few seconds, then she replied, 'All right. Tell me where he lives and we'll conclude our deal with you.'

'It's number four – ground floor – in the block of flats in Brontë Street near Paddy's Wigwam.'

'Paddy's Wigwam?'

'The Catholic cathedral. That's what the locals call it. The archbishop's called Patrick and it looks like a wigwam.'

Not realising that the nickname was affectionate,

Ruth heard only blasphemy. She shook her head sadly. 'That's another thing. The degeneration of language as well as respect for God.' Then she signalled to her minders. 'You can let him have it now.'

She turned away and walked out with the cult's scientist. She waited impassively on the waterfront beside the crane until her associates completed their business and cleaned up the scene. The only loose end – Curtis Bennett's body – was weighted down with lead piping and thrown into the Mersey.

CHAPTER 2

The effect of Anti-MP was dramatic. Doses of the drug brought the infectious stalactites and stalagmites tumbling down like dynamite crumbling a rock face in a quarry. The inflammation of the lungs and throat subsided slowly and then faded away altogether. After a few days, the only outward sign of the disease was the inevitable scar tissue and disfigurement. In the young, like Adam Satchwell, the ugly scarring would virtually disappear in time. The plastic surgeons moved in to help the severely disfigured by rebuilding mouths and noses.

The media decamped from outside the hospital, the experts from the Communicable Disease Surveillance Centre vacated the place almost before they'd broken into a sweat, and Liverpool breathed a huge sigh of relief.

That was it. Except that Inspector O'Connell hadn't been able to track Bennett's movements once he'd got out of the taxi in the city centre. And Finn had more uninvited and unwanted visitors.

151

This time, it was three heavies and one old woman. They were smartly dressed and they knocked at the door before they muscled their way in. Courteous thugs this time. It was the woman who made friends with Bouncer and, while she soothed the dog, she spoke to Finn in a curiously quiet voice. 'You've got something that doesn't belong to you.' She wasn't asking or demanding. She was stating a fact.

'I don't think so.' Finn was spread-eagled on the old chair where two of her minders had pushed him. Now, they stood on either side, intimidating him.

'A notebook. A scientific one called 7A.' The woman was oddly scary because she was so calm. Perhaps even more daunting than her male friends.

'Oh, that,' Finn replied. 'We haven't got it any more.'

The woman stopped pacing from side to side in front of him and instead gazed into his eyes. 'Are you sure? We're not in a hurry. We have the time to pull this place apart.'

Finn swallowed. 'It won't do you any good.' Shuffling nervously in the seat, he added, 'Who are you?'

Her hand came to a halt on Bouncer's neck. With anyone else, it would have been a friendly gesture. With this unruffled woman, it was threatening. Her touch on Bouncer's neck seemed to suggest that if Finn tried to deceive her, his pet would suffer as well. She ignored his question. 'Where is it now?'

'A guy called Damian took it.'

'Are you sure? We can be very . . . insistent.' Her hand lingered on Bouncer and two of the men crowded in on him.

Finn's breathing was fast and shallow. His palms were damp with sweat. 'Yes, I'm sure.'

'And who's this Damian?'

'A doctor. He called himself a germ hunter. Something like that,' he stammered.

'What's his surname and where does he work?'

Finn's hands had curled with tension into white-knuckled fists. 'Damian Brack. He works at . . . It was complicated. Something about disease surveillance.'

The woman paused, assessing him, before replying, 'Would that be the Communicable Disease Surveillance Centre?'

'Yes,' Finn answered too quickly. He just wanted to agree and get them out of his flat, out of his life.

'Are you sure?' She nodded at the two thugs.

Suddenly, they yanked him up roughly by his arms.

'You can't do this to me!' Finn cried. 'I'm going to get the freedom of the city.'

The old woman chuckled. 'Really? You've got a vivid imagination. Have you been telling me a pack of lies?'

A fist thudded into his side and he let out a yelp of pain.

Bouncer barked but didn't attempt to rescue his master.

'Telling lies is a sin,' the woman said softly, as if the thought of untruthfulness genuinely pained her.

'I'll yell and everyone'll come running.'

'No. Not in a place like this. Everyone minds their own business. Do you go to help every time a battered wife cries out? Do you go to investigate every time some kid screams in play or a fight? So,' she whispered, 'I ask you again. Where's the notebook?'

'Damian Brack's got it.'

'Is that the gospel truth?'

'Yes.'

She came right up close to study his face, but she was distracted. Her eyes flitted down to the chair where he'd been sprawled. 'What's this?' She picked up a small plastic bottle of tablets. 'Are you ill?'

Finn gasped down air. 'I got the bug that was going round. Bouncer – my dog – got it, then licked me. Sore throat and stuff. I've got to finish the pills. So's Bouncer.'

She smiled broadly. 'These are the antidote?'

'Yes.'

'That's good. Excellent, in fact.' She nodded again at her henchmen and they lowered Finn back into the chair. 'Well, thank you. You've been most . . . coopera- tive. These will do nicely.' She pocketed the little bottle of pills and, as a parting shot, said, 'It wouldn't be wise to tell anyone about our little chat, Finn. Let's keep it to ourselves.' Then she left, one minder in front and the other two behind.

Finn pulled up his shirt proudly and showed Karl the bruise on his side. It was like a trophy for living through a battle. 'It was crazy. They were packing guns as well. Sure they were.'

'Did they get them out? Threaten you with them?'

'Well, no. They'd have holsters inside their jackets. And knives.'

Trying not to be distracted by Finn's conjecture, Karl thought about the encounter some more. 'They must've been the third man's mates. Terrorists.'

'Yeah. For certain this time.'

Then it dawned on Karl. 'If they were after Notebook 7A or the antidote, it means they're trying to beat the cure. I bet they're looking at ways of turning the bug into a weapon!'

Finn hadn't thought of that, but he agreed. 'Yeah.'

'So, what are we going to do about it?'

'Nothing,' Finn answered. 'They told me to keep quiet, or . . .' He shrugged and grimaced.

'They're out of here. They were bluffing,' said Karl. 'Come on. We've got to tell that prof or Damian Brack.'

Finn didn't reply. He just looked glum.

'We can't just keep it to ourselves. You saw what this germ does. We've got to warn them.'

'How?'

'Shaughney Willett. She said her mum worked at the hospital. She'll know how to get in touch with them.'

Nurse Mollie Willett listened in shock to her daughter's friends. 'Heaven help us if you're right,' she muttered from behind the hand that covered her mouth. 'What do you want me to do? First, I'd better get you some more tablets, Finn.'

'Yes, but can you set up a meeting with Damian Brack?' Shaughney asked impatiently.

'Or Professor Monkhouse,' Karl added.

Grace stood close to Finn, regarding him as something of a hero.

Mollie nodded. 'I guess so. We've got all the contact details at work. Including a direct-line number for Damian Brack. In fact . . .' She went to her handbag and delved inside. Pulling out a small business card, she said, 'Yes. I've got it here.'

Shaughney should have been pleased, but her expression suggested resentment. 'Let's give him a call, then.'

'Now?' Mollie glanced at her watch.

'It *is* an emergency, Mum.'

Since returning from Liverpool, Damian had had a rough time. He couldn't get the loose end out of his head. The third man was out there somewhere with enough information on Eve Perry's project to make a horrifying biological weapon. If he reproduced her work but omitted the death gene from *Mycoplasma perrium*, the Liverpool outbreak would have been merely a window display for the main event. If he tailored the organism specifically for bioterrorism – rather than just let nature tinker with it – the consequences would be unimaginable.

No wonder Damian couldn't sleep. The nightmare scenario wouldn't let him.

Then a military intelligence officer called Major Hawcroft had turned up at the Communicable Disease Surveillance Centre, expressing an interest in the new life form. He told Damian and Rosalind that Inspector O'Connell had briefed him and that he would be able to help in the event of a terrorist attack. He also made it clear that he had the authority and confidence of the Government.

But Damian was suspicious about the motives of a soldier who seemed to be sniffing out a new weapon. With Rosalind's full backing, Damian had done his best to put up barriers. 'Let me show you some pictures of its victims in Liverpool,' he'd said. 'Some with exploded faces. And that's before a terrorist – or someone in the military – gets hold of it and "improves" it.'

'Believe me,' the high-ranking officer had said with a smile, 'I'm only interested in the defence of the country. Besides, you don't have a copyright on shocking injuries. We can all produce sickening slides. Do you want me to show you pictures of soldiers and civilians who've been in range of a missile or a landmine?'

'Let's be blunt. Are you trying to get hold of a biological weapon?'

Ed Hawcroft had shaken his head. 'Not for offensive purposes. But any army would want to get their hands on weapons that might be used against them. To work out a defence.'

'Defence against disease threats is *our* job,' Damian had replied tersely.

'And you do it very well, but I'm here in case of emergency. I have a lot of equipment and staff at my disposal.'

At least Damian couldn't be forced by the Government or military intelligence to hand over Dr Perry's methods because he didn't have them. The Communicable Disease Surveillance Centre had samples of *Mycoplasma perrium*, of course. They were safely stored in the unit's highest grade of biohazard laboratory, along with a supply of Anti-MP. But the bacterium with the death gene wasn't the real problem any more. The Anti-MP antidote would take care of an outbreak. Damian was losing sleep because the person with Eve Perry's detailed notes could rerun her project, making a new form of the bacterium with a different set of aims. He feared a switch from the environmentally friendly to the military.

Already nervous about the prospect, Damian wasted no time when Mollie Willett telephoned. Together with Rosalind, he set out at once for the nurse's house in Liverpool.

CHAPTER 3

There were awkward grown-up greetings all round. When Karl took the hand that Professor Rosalind Monkhouse offered him, her bracelets jangled and he felt the metallic chill of her rings contrasting with the warmth of her skin. He also noticed for the second time that she was a bit too plump.

Seeing the direction of Karl's gaze, Rosalind smiled and put her hand on her midriff. 'You're right. I've created a new life form as well. But hopefully not a new species.'

It took a few moments for Karl to grasp what she was saying. Then, stumbling over his words, he said, 'Oh, I didn't know . . . I just thought . . . Sorry. Nothing.'

Karl was saved from further embarrassment by the doorbell.

The last person to arrive was Inspector O'Connell. To Karl and Finn, he was the bore who gatecrashed and spoiled every party. But he wasn't really a gatecrasher because Rosalind had invited him.

Even though Shaughney looked sombre, Karl noted with disappointment that she seemed keen to impress

160

Damian. The germ hunter appeared rough at the edges, though. For once, he looked his age. Perhaps he'd had a heavy drinking session last night.

Finn was just Finn. There was nothing subtle happening with Finn. That's one of the things Karl admired about him. He was never devious, never clever. You got what you saw with Finn. Shuffling his door key from finger to finger, Finn told everyone what had happened to him at home and then, having lit the touchpaper, he sat back.

His words stunned the adults into silence for a few seconds.

Damian and Rosalind were the first to recognise all of the implications and react to the appalling possibility that a terrorist group was thinking of modifying *Mycoplasma perrium* for its own ends. They were particularly concerned in case fanatics removed Dr Perry's inbuilt fail-safes. More than concerned. They were visibly shaken by the idea.

Apparently struggling with the technical details, O'Connell said, 'Just paint me a picture of the consequences if this thing actually goes off.'

Rosalind took a deep breath. 'It'd be like the last outbreak but a determined terrorist could make it more infectious and deadly by adding a few well-chosen genes. If they removed the death gene, there'd be no ready-made antibiotic to kill it.'

'But you'd come up with an antidote, surely.'

Rosalind shook her head. 'They could give it genes to make it resist every antibiotic, or it'd just learn how to do it from MRSA, say, like last time. Then there'd be no known way to stop it – till it ran out of victims.'

'This time,' Damian added, 'it wouldn't be fitted with brakes.'

The police officer paused while the conjecture sank in. 'What you're saying is, it'd be attempted mass murder.'

'Genocide,' Rosalind replied.

'And this is a serious possibility?'

'With Dr Perry's notes and scientific know-how, yes.'

Under her breath, Mollie muttered, 'God forbid.'

O'Connell braced himself. 'Okay. You've given me enough ammo to get more resources out of my chief. The first thing is a fine forensic examination of your flat, Finn. We need to identify this woman and trace the third man. Top priority.' He turned back to Rosalind. 'How long have we got? If someone's started working on this biological weapon, how long before they could use it?'

Rosalind shrugged. 'Not long. If they've got a decent biologist on the job, they could do it in a matter of days because they wouldn't bother with all the scientific niceties of checking and testing of results. They could blunder through in a couple of weeks, maybe.'

'Right. Finn, I want you to come with me and see a specialist in facial recognition. He'll help you come up with a likeness of that woman – and any of the men you can remember.'

'But . . .'

'Don't worry. You'll enjoy it. It's not about Identikits – sketching different noses any more – it's an e-fit system: building features from a computerised library.'

'What about us?' Shaughney's mum asked, looking at Damian. 'There was an outside chance, you said, that Shaughney and me are immune. You could use us to make a vaccine.'

'There *was* a chance,' he replied, stressing the past tense. 'But when we got around to your saliva samples . . .' He shook his head. 'No, you don't have natural immunity. You were just lucky not to carry it to your mouths.'

Inspector O'Connell ended the discussion by emphasising the need to keep everything quiet. He certainly didn't want to have to battle with reporters and a panicked public as well as a possible terrorist gang with a weapon as potent as a nuclear device.

On Friday, Finn was full of himself. He still had a yellowy-brown bruise to show off and now he'd been in the cop shop without being a suspect. He'd assembled a jigsaw of that sinister woman from bits and pieces stored in the police computer. He'd become a virtual Frankenstein by putting together body parts and he couldn't possibly keep it to himself.

He picked up a stone from the path and chucked it into the Mersey. He listened for the splash and watched the impression that he'd made on the world.

Bouncer had caught the bug by licking Weston Smith's face but Anti-MP had also worked on him. Fully fit again, the Alsatian tugged on his lead to reach the tantalising smells of a litter bin.

Grace remarked, 'He does like his scents, doesn't he?'

'Scent! Stink is more like it.' Finn looked down at the loop of leather tightening around his wrist and came to a halt.

'What is it?' Grace said.

'Oh, nothing. It doesn't matter,' Finn replied, dragging Bouncer away and carrying on with the walk. 'Just that one of them was wearing a wristband.'

'Who?'

'One of those blokes. I saw it when he grabbed me. I didn't worry about it – just one of those charity thingies, but . . .' He shook his head. He couldn't figure out what was bothering him, but he knew that something wasn't quite right.

Karl helped him out. 'Bullies don't support charity.'

'Yeah. That's it. Anyway, it had a cross on it and some letters. FCR or something like.'

Grace looked shocked. 'A cross? As in crucifixion, you mean?' Her hand went to the place above her chest where a crucifix hung under her coat.

'I suppose so.'

164

'Was it pale orange?'

'Yeah.'

'I've seen one of those. Any chance the letters were FRC?' she said.

'Yeah.'

'Why?' Karl asked. 'What's FRC?'

'A cult,' Grace replied with disdain. 'Religious nuts. If you thought the Catholic Church was strict, you ought to try those guys. Fundamentalist Revolutionary Church. Weird lot, from what I hear.'

Finn looked bemused.

Karl said, 'If this bloke was religious, why did he punch someone?'

'Not just someone. Me,' Finn muttered.

'Yeah. Why would someone religious beat Finn up? Aren't you supposed to be nice to others?'

Grace sniffed. 'Yes, but . . . I said they were weird. If you want to beat people up, you can always find a fire-and-brimstone section of the Bible to justify it. They're the eye-for-an-eye brigade.'

Karl thought about it for a moment. 'Where do they meet? And when?'

Grace shrugged. 'I can find out. There's a girl at school . . . Joanne. Her parents are in it. She's really fed up. She says they've given just about all their worldly goods to the sect. Jo's left with next to nothing.' She paused before adding, 'Shouldn't you tell the police?'

Finn and Karl shook their heads in unison. 'Nah. Let's see what *we* can find out first,' Karl said.

'You mean, let's see what *I* can find out.'

'Yeah, that's right,' Finn agreed.

Grace hesitated and then smiled at him. 'Okay. I'll come to your place after school on Monday and tell you what I've got.'

It was a long and difficult Monday at school. Their brains weren't really in the right gear. Still, double Science was a riot because Mr Dee was off sick and the supply teacher was a pushover.

At break, Finn said, 'I've been thinking . . .'

'Dangerous,' Karl interrupted with a smile.

'No, it's this O'Connell fella. He doesn't seem so bad.'

'What?' Karl exclaimed. 'I never thought I'd hear you being nice about the police.'

'Yeah, well.'

Karl guessed that his friend was about to suggest that they should go to the police. 'Forget it. We don't need help.' He paused before adding, 'Look. We did pretty well on our own with the notebooks – well, one of them. We saved lots of people. We cured it. Just you and me. Heroes.'

'You want us to be superheroes now.'

'Yeah. Superheroes versus the superbug. We'd be magnets to girls as well.' Karl waited till some boys had rushed past, chasing a football. 'But I reckon finding the leader of this cult is no good. Maybe she's a crank, but she's not the big issue. What we want is their tame scientist. He's got our lab book . . .'

'Our?' Finn queried.

'Yeah. Eve Perry gave it to us. Anyway, we find him – or her – and grab it back. End of panic. They're stuck without it. They must have a lab or whatever somewhere. We've just got to find it.'

Finn grimaced. 'As easy as nailing custard to a wall.'

'You wouldn't have a problem with my mum's,' Karl replied. 'It's way beyond lumpy.'

CHAPTER 4

It was dawn on Sunday and the members of the Fundamentalist Revolutionary Church had gathered, just as Grace had said they would, on the vast stretch of sand that capped north Wirral, on the other side of the Mersey. There were about thirty people, wrapped up well, on the beach between West Kirby and the tiny islands of Hilbre.

Later in the day, when the sun was higher and the tide lower, some walkers and joggers would make for the islands and aim to get back before the incoming sea cut them off. Right now, the wet sand was deserted apart from the FRC cluster, one early-morning dog-walker and his lumbering Labrador.

Karl and Finn had not reached the beach in time to see the congregation arriving. They'd never been up so early on a Sunday. And they'd never seen such a weird church. They were used to a concrete wigwam, but not to the open air. Still, it made a kind of sense to Karl. If people wanted to worship God and praise His good work, it was logical to be in the midst of it at the time. Even so, it seemed bizarre. From the car-park on South

Parade, the cult looked like a bunch of tourists about to go sightseeing. A tour guide seemed to be addressing them before they set off on their weekend ramble.

Crouching behind a Peugeot, the boys could not make out individuals, but it was likely that the cult's scientist was in the flock. Grace had told them that the sect was very strict about not working on Sundays and that all FRC members attended every service. Karl and Finn could probably see him or her right now. But there was no way of knowing which one he was. Besides, the group was too far away to pick out a particular person. Apart from the woman at the front.

Finn was certain that the leader was the woman who had gatecrashed his flat and taken away his Anti-MP pills. He guessed that some smart guys standing at the back were her henchmen as well but he couldn't be certain.

Karl was not sure what he expected to get out of this bit of snooping. He didn't know what he could learn from spying on the strange church service, but nosying around seemed the right thing to do. He hoped to see something that would point them in the right direction. Until he'd tried and failed, he wasn't ready to hand the job over to O'Connell and his team.

The police had been on the job all week and still had nothing to show except a good likeness of the cult's leader and a load of microscopic clues from Finn's flat, but no real results. They had identified the third Green

Warrior as Curtis Bennett, but that was handed to them on a plate when his parents reported him missing. Apparently, Bennett had been behaving oddly since losing his job at a chemical factory and the police found evidence of online gambling debts on his computer. His mother and father were worried for his life and O'Connell had him marked down as a potential suicide.

Karl was hoping that, when the followers trudged back to dry land from the beach, he'd get a good look at them. But it was dangerous. He wouldn't be able to hide with Finn behind the Peugeot because it probably belonged to someone in the FRC. One-by-one, all of the parked cars would pull away, leaving Karl and Finn exposed. When the service finished, they planned to move to the nearby shop and peer round the brickwork to get a view of the departing worshippers.

According to Grace's contact – Joanne – it was all doom and gloom with the fringe church at the moment. Her mum and dad hadn't said why. They just looked glum all the time. The atmosphere of the distant meeting seemed to reflect that mood. The members of the Fundamentalist Revolutionary Church huddled together grimly and their coats flapped about in the sea breeze. Finn and Karl didn't know what was being said on the sand but the meeting certainly wasn't a joyous occasion with singing and happy clapping.

When the Sunday service finally broke up, Karl and

Finn took up a discreet position by the shop. They squatted down and waited, eyes glued to the stationary cars.

The first people to emerge onto South Parade were two middle-aged couples. They talked to each other for a few seconds, then strolled to their cars and drove away. Within quarter of an hour, almost all of the FRC members had come up from the sand and departed. The trickle of cars had nearly dried up. The only people who lingered were the leader, three of her heavies and another man with his back to the boys. He could have been the missing protester but Finn and Karl didn't have a hope of identifying him. He got into the back of a four-by-four with tinted windows. The woman stood by the front passenger's door and chatted earnestly for a while to her henchmen. One of them seemed to be nervous. He kept on glancing around, surveying the scene for signs of trouble.

With pounding hearts, the boys pulled back behind the corner of the shop.

When two more doors thudded shut, they dared to peer out again. The nervous minder was about to get into the driver's seat. The woman hesitated, looked around for the final time and adjusted her coat. Then she got in and slammed the door. Almost at once, the four-wheel-drive took off down the road in the direction of Hoylake.

Disappointed, Karl and Finn came out from their

hiding place. Karl put both fists on his waist and let out a long breath. 'Bugger!' he muttered irritably.

Finn nodded. 'What a waste of time that was. I could've had four or five more hours in bed.'

They began to stroll back to where the cars had been parked – now almost deserted – when Karl cocked his head on one side. 'Hang on! What's that?'

Where the leader had rearranged her coat before climbing into the car, there was a small white card on the kerb. At once, Karl guessed that it had fluttered unnoticed from one of her pockets. He bent down, grabbed it and exclaimed, 'Yes!'

'What?'

'Look. A sort of business card.'

Across the top was written *Fundamentalist Revolutionary Church*. Underneath was a website address, a telephone number, and a postal address in Meols Drive, Hoylake.

'Bingo!' Finn cried.

'And it's near here, I think. Meols Drive is the main road back to Birkenhead. Come on. We can walk it.'

There was a collection of five great big posh places just off the main road through Hoylake. The estate was so exclusive, it had a big gate to keep out riff-raff like Finn and Karl. Hidden from the boys, the fronts of the houses were facing the other way, as if they'd turned their backs on the ordinary folk using the road.

Karl and Finn had ducked behind a bush on Meols Drive and they watched as a car swept into the private entrance. They didn't see much apart from the driver's hand poking out of the window and punching a number into a keypad, followed by the tall gate sliding aside silently. Once the car had glided into the inner sanctum, a hidden mechanism pushed the gate shut like an iron curtain.

'I've heard about this,' Finn whispered.

'How do you mean?'

'The golf course is on the other side of these houses. When there's a big tournament on – like the Open or whatever it's called – people round here leave home for a couple of weeks and charge golf nuts the earth – thousands – to stay here and watch the action from their front rooms.'

Karl smiled. 'We should rent out our flats to people who want to watch drug pushers.' He paused before adding, 'The cops might cough up quite a bit for a spot of surveillance from my bedroom. Perhaps I should have a chat with O'Connell . . .' He stopped talking as a car pulled up on the other side of the gate and waited for it to roll gently back.

After the BMW had gone, Finn said quietly, 'Now what? We're still not getting anywhere. We don't even know which one's the right number.'

Karl nodded. Glancing at the business card, he said, 'We want number five.' He slipped the card back into his pocket, then broke into a smile. 'Here's an idea.'

'What?'

'If they can watch golf from the other side, we could spy on them from the golf course.'

'Good thinking,' Finn replied. 'What are we waiting for?'

CHAPTER 5

From the rough by the sixth hole, Karl and Finn peered through the branches at the nearest house. It was at least ten times the size of their apartments and it had a fancy balcony around its first floor. They were sure it was the sect's headquarters because the four-by-four with tinted windows was parked outside.

Karl said, 'If all the people give their money to this cult thing, like Joanne's folks, I suppose they can afford a place like this.' The boys couldn't get very close to it because of the hedgerow and fence at the edge of the golf course, but there was no sign of life. No one appeared at the front door or any of the windows, and the ample garden was empty. Karl and Finn had a view of a turning circle and a couple of parked cars, but that was the only advantage of seeing the house from the golf course.

Karl sighed.

Finn poked him with an elbow.

'What?'

'See? The other car. The red one.'

'Mmm. Ferrari. Nice.'

'More than nice,' Finn replied. 'It's the same as Mr Dee's.'

Karl looked at the car again and then at his mate. 'You're right. Does that mean . . .?'

'What?'

'Is it Mr Dee's? Was that who we saw at West Kirby? He's not the cult's scientist, is he? I thought it'd be Bennett – the one who did a runner with our lab book.'

Finn shrugged. 'Mr Dee? Shouldn't think so. He's a teacher.'

'I don't think the teachers' rule book says they can't be God-botherers.'

'But he's off ill.'

Karl laughed quietly. 'Are you always ill when you tell the school you are?'

'Yeah, but . . . He's a teacher. He's supposed to . . .'

'Tell the truth?'

'Yeah.'

Two men walked out onto the balcony and the boys squeezed themselves behind a tree trunk at the edge of the rough. Peering out cautiously, Finn watched the two men part and amble to either end of the lavish terrace. They didn't seem to be watching golf. They were lookouts.

'They're two of the heavies who barged into my flat!'

'Sure?'

'Pretty much.'

'Well, we can't move without them seeing. And we don't look like golfers. So we're stuck.'

'Sod it.'

'It's all right,' Karl replied, his back against the rough bark. 'We're going to hang around anyway.'

'Are we?'

'Yeah. Wait and see who drives the Ferrari away. We'd recognise Mr Dee from here if it's him. Or we'd see it's someone else.'

The boys slumped down till they were sitting shoulder-to-shoulder at the base of the tree trunk.

After about ten minutes, the guards on patrol went back inside, allowing Karl and Finn to relax. They flattened themselves on the ground, lying on their stomachs, chins resting on their crossed arms. Karl's head was poking out from behind the tree on the left with Finn on the right. It was cold, but at least the earth was dry and it wasn't pouring with rain. To their right, the golf course stretched all the way back to West Kirby.

After an hour and a half, there was still no movement and the red Ferrari just sat there, as if it were part of a computer game on pause.

Karl groaned and shook his head.

'There goes your plan,' Finn said. 'Unless we make camp for the day.'

'We'll get chucked out sooner or later. Some bloke with a putter and dodgy trousers will report us.'

Finn nodded towards the house that was nearly a mansion. 'Maybe it's Dee's place.'

'Nah. He lives back over the water somewhere, I'm pretty sure. In the city. They don't pay teachers enough for something like this. Bet he blew all his money on his car. And look at the size of the garage. It's as big as our two flats put together. That's where you'd put a Ferrari if you lived here.'

'Maybe it's got nothing to do with Mr Dee, then.'

Karl nodded. 'Maybe.' He took a deep breath and then looked at his mate. 'What do you reckon if we come back after dark . . .'

Interrupting, Finn said, 'No way. It'd be easier to break into a bank.'

'It's not that bad,' Karl replied.

Finn pointed. 'That's a pretty big fence to climb over.'

'There's a hedge near the gate at the front. We hide there till someone opens the gate and we dash through before it closes. There was a few seconds after a car goes in.'

'I bet there's cameras and a burglar alarm.'

'Cover up with a hoodie. I only want to get a closer look at the car. If it's Mr Dee's, it'll have a school pass on the windscreen.'

'Oh, yeah. I never thought of that. Well, if it's only the car you're after, I'm up for it.'

'Might have to do a bit of climbing on the way out – unless someone turns up at the right time and opens the gate, but don't bank on it.'

Finn eyed the tall wire fence. 'Tricky but . . .'

'We've done worse things.'

Finn sniffed. 'All right. Count me in.'

At seven-thirty, Finn and Karl were loitering in some bushes on Meols Drive, waiting for the large gate to slide back whenever a legitimate visitor made an entrance. It could all happen in the next five seconds or it might take five hours. They had to be ready to run through the narrowing gap at any moment and hope that they weren't caught on closed-circuit TV or spotted in a rear-view mirror.

Their plan was to dash through the security gate and head directly for the cluster of poplars to the left of the house with the Ferrari. The trees would provide them with cover.

They got to try the idea at ten past eight. When a brand new Lexus rolled sedately up to the gate, they both took a deep breath and readied themselves like sprinters on starting blocks. An arm emerged from the driver's window, the hand punched in a code and the gate began to open. Nearby, there was a smooth whirring sound.

'Ready?' Karl whispered.

Finn nodded.

As soon as the gate drew back enough, the silver Lexus coasted into the private estate.

'Wait a second,' Finn said. 'Or they'll see us.'

The gate juddered very slightly as it came to a stop, fully open. It was motionless for a few seconds but then, somehow sensing the car moving away, it started to close.

Karl's heart was thumping madly. 'We've got to . . .'

Finn took charge because this was what he was good at. He put up his palm. When the gate reached its half-way point, he said, 'Now!' Leading the charge, he leapt into action with Karl a second or two behind him.

As soon as they trod on the tarmac, their trainers got a good grip and they accelerated towards the ever-shrinking entry. Overtaking the gate, Finn skidded a little as he changed angle and darted through the opening. The Lexus disappeared around the corner. Luckily, its brake lights didn't turn the night air blood red. All the time, the moving iron framework lessened the breach in the estate's defences. Karl hesitated, turned sideways and slipped through before the hole closed up entirely and the gate shuddered to a stop.

'Phew!' Finn whispered among the evergreens.

Karl patted his flat stomach. 'Good job I haven't eaten yet,' he replied in a hush. 'Come on. Down the road. There's no windows overlooking it.'

They tiptoed down the smart block-paved drive, sneaking noiselessly round to the other side of the house where the sports car was parked in front of the golf course – now in darkness. There were no distant lights because, beyond the greens, there was nothing but the beach and Liverpool Bay. Karl guessed that there was an idyllic view in daylight from the upstairs rooms. Very different from the sights on offer from his own flat.

The boys paused at the corner of the house. Another step and they'd be in sight of the balcony and several windows. Decorative lamps attached to the brickwork meant that they could be seen. Attached to the garage and over the back door, there were also security lights with movement detectors. As soon as they stepped towards the turning circle, the powerful beams would probably come on.

'Well?' Finn murmured.

Karl scratched his head. 'Make a dash for it? Get close enough to see the windscreen, then run back and over the gate?'

'Are you sure?'

'It's that or give up right now.'

'Okay,' Finn replied. 'Let's do it.'

But they never did get a good look at the Ferrari. They tore out of the shadows into a sudden blaze of security spotlights. Blinded by the glare, they ran straight into the strong arms of the cult's waiting minders.

CHAPTER 6

Before they knew it, Finn and Karl were tied to chairs with their ankles chained to the floor in the basement of the large house. But it wasn't like a normal cellar. It wasn't damp, or filled with wine racks, or a dumping ground for unused bits and pieces, or a mass of pipes, wires and woodlice. It was an immaculate fully-fitted laboratory, rather like Eve Perry's room at the university, but far neater and more modern. Presumably, it had been funded by donations from members of the Fundamentalist Revolutionary Church.

And standing alongside the biological equipment was Mr Dee, wearing a white lab coat. He was smiling, yet it wasn't a happy smile. He didn't appear to be amused or angry, but he did look pleased. His wry expression suggested that his pupils' intrusion was more a godsend than a nuisance.

'I wish you'd shown as much initiative and enthusiasm as this in class,' he said, shaking his head. 'You'd have got a lot more marks. Here, you get the chance to be guinea-pigs.'

At one end of the clean and sterile lab, there were

cages containing real guinea-pigs. There were mice, rats and rabbits, too. They all looked strangely subdued in the unnatural environment.

Karl felt subdued as well. The plastic ties holding his hands together behind the chair dug into his skin and the science teacher's comment sounded sinister. 'What do you mean?' he asked.

'You'll see.'

The sect's leader came out from behind the boys in a long flowing white dress like a fashionable lab coat. Halting in front of them, she asked softly, 'Why are you here?'

'Who are you?' Karl said.

'Finn knows perfectly well. Don't you? We've bumped into each other before. You may call me Ruth. Now, answer the question, please.'

Finn shuffled on his chair, grimacing at the twinges in his wrists. 'The police know you as well now. They've got an e-fit.'

She smiled. 'Plucking my appearance out of your memory is a long way from turning up at the front door.'

'We did,' said Karl. 'We told the police where . . .'

She chuckled. 'Forgive me, but you don't seem to me to be the sort of boys who keep the police force informed of your whereabouts and your bright ideas. And you don't have mobile phones on you. We checked. So, tell me, why did you come here?'

183

Karl couldn't see any reason to avoid the truth. 'We came for the lab book.' He nodded towards a desk where he'd already seen it. 'It's ours. She gave it us.'

Ruth gazed at him for a few seconds, then said, 'How did you hear about our meeting for worship?'

'We were walking along the beach and . . .'

It was Mr Dee's turn to laugh. 'Come on, Karl. You can do better than that.'

Suddenly realising that he'd been tricked, Karl said, 'You saw us at West Kirby and dropped the business card on purpose, didn't you? You *wanted* us to come.'

Ruth smiled again. 'You took the bait, yes. But I won't let you avoid my question.'

Annoyed that he'd been duped so easily, Karl let out a sigh. 'We know someone in your . . . organisation.'

'Who?'

Karl shook his head.

'Who?' Ruth repeated.

'Well, we don't really,' Karl answered. Determined to protect Grace and Joanne, he continued with a lie. 'Just the son of one of your people.'

'And his surname is . . .?'

Karl shook his head again.

Mr Dee stepped forward. 'Believe me, Ruth. They won't tell you. It's a code of honour among kids. They don't tell on each other. Ever. A nuisance, but that's the way it is.'

Ruth nodded. Addressing Karl and Finn, she said,

'I'm not sure that's my idea – or God's idea – of honour, but I'll let it pass. It has some merit. An element of respect for your peers.' She walked to and fro, thinking, and then came to a sudden halt. 'It doesn't matter. Your anonymous friend can guide the police to the beach but he isn't going to lead a cavalry charge here. No one in the church will ever reveal this address. Anyway, our experiments are drawing to a conclusion. This will be your last home before Judgement.'

Karl and Finn exchanged a worried glance.

Ruth smiled. 'No need to look like that. The hour of Judgement is great news – for the righteous. It's when God calls us to account and delivers peace to His servants who have suffered so much in this loveless, wicked society.' Before Karl could ask her a question, she turned abruptly and walked away. At the door, she said dryly to Mr Dee, 'Continue.'

Karl switched his gaze to the teacher. 'What are you going to do to us?'

'You should feel privileged,' Mr Dee replied. 'You've been chosen for this, not by me, but by God.'

Without warning, Mr Dee grabbed Karl's jaw with one hand, forcing his mouth open. He put two pills on Karl's tongue with his other hand. Then he closed his student's mouth and pinched his nose to make him swallow.

'What was . . .?' Karl gasped.

Expertly, the teacher did the same to Finn. Then he

explained, 'It's what they give you in hospital before taking you off for an operation. They're sedatives to make you relaxed and cooperative. You see, we don't want any histrionics.'

Karl repeated his question. 'What are you going to do to us?'

'We needed at least one human subject. We asked for a volunteer among our own, but then God sent you instead.' He paused before quoting, 'Abraham built an altar there and stretched forth his hand to slay his son, but an angel of the Lord said, "Lay not thine hand upon the lad. Behold a ram caught in the thicket by its horns." So Abraham took the ram and offered it as a burnt offering instead of his son.'

'You've cracked,' Karl shouted at him.

'What's this about offering and stuff?' Finn said.

Mr Dee walked over to the desk and tapped the laboratory notebook. 'You see, I'm not as clever as Dr Perry. I needed her instructions. And they're beautifully clear. They've made it possible for an ordinary biologist like me to do extraordinary things. I'm the third person to make life on Earth. God first and foremost, then Eve Perry, and now me. Dr Perry was brilliant, but wayward. I'm run-of-the-mill up here,' he said, pointing to the side of his head, 'but fundamentally good because, as I said to you once before, I conduct science in the service of God.'

'What science?'

Mr Dee waved towards the far end of the laboratory where there was a door with a biohazard sign. 'I've modified *Mycoplasma perrium* for God's purpose. I suppose you'd call it *Mycoplasma perrium-dee*. It can infect humans and it carries a gene that'll make it release a poison. I've also removed its death gene. Experiments with mice tell me Anti-MP doesn't have an effect on it any more. If that's true with people as well, it's the most deadly weapon against humans I can think of.'

Karl cried, 'You're going to give us the disease to make sure this Anti-MP doesn't work!'

Mr Dee nodded. 'You have that honour, yes.'

'What's the point?' Karl asked, trying to stay focused, trying to keep fear at bay. 'What are you going to do with it?'

'Nothing,' Mr Dee said with a warped smile. 'Just open the doors and let God decide. He'll choose who's worthy and who isn't. He'll settle humanity's fate. Maybe we'll be spared, maybe we won't. He might decide we've blown our one and only chance. He might decide to use the germ as His instrument of retribution.'

'You've definitely cracked,' Finn mumbled.

Mr Dee ignored Finn. Glancing from one boy to the other, he said, 'The question is, who's going to be the first host, and the first martyr?'

CHAPTER 7

Rosalind Monkhouse leaned forward and her features went out of focus for a moment. Reaching out to adjust the camcorder, her face was briefly distorted and threateningly large. Then she sat back and everything returned to normal. Her head and shoulders were central again. She exhaled and continued her commentary in a more personal, less scientific style.

'It was last Sunday – the twenty-seventh of March – when Finn Pallister and Karl Stephenson disappeared, and we all knew what it meant. Straightaway, I made the decision to withdraw to headquarters. You see, I'd been thinking about what to do if it came to this. I decided the only place for me was here in the high-containment lab, with a sample of *Mycoplasma perrium*. My reasoning was simple. If a terrorist group unleashed it as a weapon, I could carry on working towards a cure while keeping safe in here. I *must* remain healthy if I'm going to beat this bacterium. I must avoid contact with it at all costs because I might be the only one who stands a chance of defeating it. Being here's the best – the only – way I can help. If I died . . .' She shrugged.

'Scientists are trained to be meticulous about keeping

records. I'm putting all my findings on computer and I'm making this video, spelling out everything I know, in case . . . But I'm not going to think the worst. Not while there's hope.

'Anyway, here I am, forced back to the coal-face, with the danger under control. I've removed the death gene from *Mycoplasma perrium* because that's the first thing a terrorist would do. My main aim now is to find a way of defeating this potential weapon. It's not easy. I'm taking modafinil every day to keep exhaustion at bay, allowing me to work around the clock as much as possible. Existing on stimulants isn't the most responsible way for a pregnant woman to behave, but I don't have much choice.' She glanced to the side, then added, 'My provisions of water, food and drugs will last for a little while longer. I'm not at crisis point yet.'

Professor Rosalind Monkhouse's meticulous report was becoming a poignant video diary.

CHAPTER 8

Rumours about Finn Pallister and Karl Stephenson began to circulate on Monday. They weren't at home and they didn't go to school. Everyone who knew them shrugged and said, 'Well, what do you expect? Finn and Karl, eh?' Inspector O'Connell's attitude was different. Listening to Grace Fordham talking about Finn, an outfit called the Fundamentalist Revolutionary Church and its outdoor meetings in West Kirby, the detective grew increasingly concerned for the missing boys.

He was also grateful to Grace for his first solid lead. At once, he saturated the coastal town on the Wirral with police officers and forensic specialists. He also took Joanne and her parents into custody and questioned them endlessly about the cult. But he got nothing out of them. Joanne's mother and father were as silent as Trappist monks. Joanne knew about the FRC's Sunday services – because her parents encouraged her to attend – but nothing else about the fringe church. As O'Connell's anxiety grew, he ordered helicopter surveillance of the river estuaries, Liverpool

Bay and north Wirral. By Tuesday, though, he was no wiser.

First, Curtis Bennett had vanished from the face of the planet and now Finn and Karl seemed to be following in his footsteps. The two lads had probably acted like typical boys. They'd got wind of a morsel of intelligence from Grace and then, full of bravado, they'd almost certainly waded into something that was far too deep for them, instead of leaving it to the professionals. O'Connell was very worried for their well-being.

Then there was Professor Monkhouse. She'd gone back to work in an underground laboratory where she could be isolated from the rest of the world. He could contact her by phone, email and video conferencing, but it wasn't the same as having a recognised authority on hand. She'd left an undoubtedly courageous but inexperienced Damian Brack in charge.

And every hour that passed, O'Connell had to assume that the terrorists would be sixty minutes closer to perfecting and maybe even releasing a lethal weapon that could be passed around unseen like flu. Rosalind's words echoed in his brain. 'If they've got a decent biologist on the job, they could do it in a matter of days. They could blunder through in a couple of weeks, maybe.' She'd said that a week last Thursday: twelve days ago.

He sat at his desk and stared ahead. Like a rabbit

transfixed by oncoming headlights, he couldn't see a rational way out of the situation.

Finn and Karl were caged in a covert laboratory just off Meols Drive, like experimental animals waiting to be sacrificed for the sake of scientific progress.

'Just imagine,' Mr Dee said to them on Monday. 'A superbug that thrives in the community, that's immune to all antibiotics, without a cure. It amounts to a modern-day epidemic. And God has put it in my hands. He wouldn't have done that unless He knew I'd do the right thing with it. He knows I'll release it. So, that proves it's God's will.' He began to climb into an all-over protective suit similar to the one they'd seen hanging in Eve Perry's laboratory.

Karl cringed. 'That's no proof. I thought you were supposed to be a scientist.'

Mr Dee hesitated. 'You're right. It's a mix of proof and faith. But I don't expect you to understand that. I'm going to give the world what it needs: a clean slate for God to work with. Like the extinction of the dinosaurs, or Noah's flood. It's time for a different form of evolution. Survival of the godliest.' He busied himself with sealing his suit.

Karl twisted his head to look at Finn, the most dependable friend he'd ever had. 'You and me. We've done some daft things, had some good times.'

Finn nodded but couldn't summon a smile.

'Do you remember Sadie?'

Finn frowned and shook his head. He looked drowsy.

'You do. She was getting knocked about at school because she looked gay.'

'Oh, her.'

'What was your idea to stop her getting hurt?'

'Thump 'em. The bullies.'

Karl managed a faint smile. 'Direct action. As always with you. Boisterous but kind. You'd have been excluded for walloping girls.' His speech was slower and quieter than normal. Every sentence required effort.

'Didn't you start a rumour you'd had sex with her?' Finn mumbled.

Ignoring Mr Dee, Karl nodded. 'Did us both a lot of good. They didn't pick on her any more. Job done.'

'You were always smart.' Finn paused for several seconds, his eyes half closed, before he asked, 'Do you think she *was* gay?'

Karl shrugged, jolting his bound wrists. 'Never thought about it. Bet she hadn't either. Doesn't matter.'

'Yeah. What matters is, you got her out of a hole.'

Karl looked around the basement and then back at his immobilised friend. 'Sorry, Finn. I'm right out of smart ideas.'

Looking like a spaceman, Mr Dee came up to him. The teacher didn't have to say a word.

Karl had volunteered to go first to give his friend a bit more of a chance, a few more hours or days. Finn deserved it. Karl knew that's what his mate would've wanted. But if the FRC was about to release a devastating biological weapon, Karl preferred to be at the head of the queue. He didn't see any point in lingering around to witness everyone else's misery and death.

Mr Dee unlocked the chain that tethered Karl's ankle to the ground. Then he grabbed Karl's arm – still tied behind his back – and lifted him from the seat.

Karl's limp legs didn't take his weight straightaway. He staggered and almost fell, but the teacher steadied him and led him towards the door with the biohazard warning. He felt like a drowsy prisoner being guided to the gallows.

Karl looked over his shoulder at Finn, but he couldn't say anything. His mouth was suddenly too dry and his brain had gone into some sort of paralysis. That was probably the effect of the sedatives. At the far end of the lab, a couple of bouncers were on hand in case the boys gave Mr Dee any trouble.

Finn screamed defiantly, 'No!' Still trying to resist the drugs that Mr Dee fed them every few hours, Finn banged a foot on the floor, rattling the chain that kept him rooted to the spot. But his protest came to a premature end and he simply looked helpless.

The heavy door opened slowly and a light came on in a pure white and claustrophobic tunnel. It was about five paces long, with another sealed door at the end. When Karl shuffled inside, it was a bit like walking into a large fridge. He felt dreadfully cold. Clearly, it was an airlock, a limbo that was neither part of the clean world that he'd just left nor contaminated like the ominous room ahead of him. Above him in the ceiling, there were shower heads and below there was a drain that would take away contaminated water. Treatment with strong acid or concentrated bleach probably awaited. It was a pity, Karl thought, that infected people couldn't be treated in the same way, but the fatal bug would be inside their bodies and the chemicals would be as deadly as the disease.

Behind him, Mr Dee had a small cylinder of air incorporated within his suit. Karl could hear its sinister hiss as his science teacher breathed in. There was no such supply of clean air for Karl.

Mr Dee waved him forward. His muffled voice said, 'Stand to one side. I'll open the door.'

For a moment, Karl thought of attacking Mr Dee, but with his wrists bound behind his back and sedatives flowing through his veins, he didn't have a lot of options. Besides, there were those two heavies in the room behind him, and he couldn't free Finn without the key to the padlock that secured the chain. Also, he knew that if he kicked out at the teacher and ran from the tunnel, he might let the biological weapon loose. He would never want responsibility for that.

195

Mr Dee opened the final door to reveal a small windowless room like a larder. On shelves to the right and left, there were racks of petri dishes and a few small cages containing disfigured and bleeding mice. Some of the poor creatures with burst faces and matted fur seemed to be dead. On a small table, there was a supply of drinking water, some sandwiches sealed in a plastic container and Finn's bottle of Anti-MP tablets.

Karl felt a push in the small of his back and he slumped lethargically into the only chair.

Now, Mr Dee's voice came out of a speaker. 'You should feel privileged to be a servant of the Lord.'

'Huh.'

'It's an honour to be chosen.'

Karl's thoughts had been splintered by the sedative. It took him a while to piece together what he wanted to say. 'Strange you had to drug me when it's such an honour.'

Mr Dee ignored his slurred words. 'You may well be infected with the instrument of retribution already. Your very first breath in this room might have been enough. I'll see how you get on and talk to you from out there.' He jerked his head towards the tunnel, then pointed upwards at two cameras set high in the wall. There was a speaker, microphone and bright light as well. All of them were out of Karl's reach.

'You're going to watch me get ill and go downhill.'

'I'm going to tell you when to take the Anti-MP pills.' He tapped the plastic bottle on the table.

'What if I refuse?'

Inside his protective suit, Mr Dee shrugged as if he didn't care. 'I'll force-feed them to you, if necessary. Other than that, you just hasten the time when your best friend takes your place.'

Karl was powerless to stop a tear running down his cheek. 'How long will this take?' Choking over his words, he asked, 'How long have I got?'

Mr Dee bent down and undid the tie around Karl's wrists. With his fingers wrapped in thick latex, he was somewhat clumsy. 'I really don't know. It'll be quicker than the Liverpool outbreak because I've improved it. It's more infectious and it produces a toxin now. If it's valid to extrapolate from rats and rabbits, it'll take between twenty-four and forty-eight hours. Before then, we'll see what happens when you take the tablets.' He stepped back and, before he left, he asked, 'Anything else you want to ask before . . .?'

Karl stared at the man behind the plastic mask. He wanted to say so much. He wanted to fly into a rage, to rip his protective suit and take the teacher down with him, but strangely the fury wouldn't come. Anyway, fighting and infecting Mr Dee seemed pointless when he was about to prove that his bacterium was a supreme weapon. Like everyone else, he'd be exposed to *Mycoplasma perrium-dee* soon enough. Then he would find out what his God thought of him.

Or would he? Still struggling to put together a

sentence, Karl asked, 'When you let this thing out, where will you be?'

'Out there, waiting. I'm no different. I'll face God's judgement as well.'

'What about Ruth?'

Mr Dee frowned. 'The same.'

'Sure she hasn't booked a ticket to Australia?'

There was a split-second delay before he laughed at the idea. 'That's ludicrous. Anyway, nowhere will be safe.'

Karl paused again. 'A small island no one's heard of or goes to?'

'You're trying to sow the seeds of distrust amongst us, that's all. Good try under the circumstances, but save your breath for prayer.'

'I just don't know how you can . . . You'll go down as the world's worst killer . . .'

Mr Dee interrupted. 'And it's saviour.'

Karl's head drooped. When he looked up, his eyes were wet again and his nose was running. 'You got to drive a Ferrari. Not like me. You're not giving me the same chances you had.'

Mr Dee turned and walked awkwardly away. His voice made a tutting noise in the loudspeaker. 'Ferraris aren't important. Greed for material goods and wealth is all part of the problem.'

When the teacher left and sealed the door, Karl could hear water surging through pipes. No doubt, Mr Dee was showering away the contamination in the tunnel. Afterwards, a pump chugged for several minutes, probably sucking away the tainted air before Mr Dee could safely re-enter the normal world.

As soon as Karl could summon the courage and strength, he looked around his final home. It wasn't much to boast about. With his hands free, he could trash the place. But the sedative sapped his willpower and no amount of damage would serve a purpose. Doubtless, the experiment could continue in a wrecked room. With its cages of horrible dead and dying animals, and its petri dishes smeared with the biological weapon, the small space embodied everything that Weston Smith and Angus Kerven had tried to prevent.

Karl coughed and put his head in his hands. He thought of his mum and dad, Shaughney with her giant earrings, Rosalind Monkhouse and young Adam Satchwell. And he thought of Finn, unknowingly waiting his turn outside. Karl knew that Finn would be sacrificed next because, no matter what the outcome of this first experiment with a human being, Mr Dee would want to repeat it to make sure of the result. Whatever else Mr Dee was, he was also a scientist.

Where was Karl's fighting spirit when he'd needed it most? It had been crushed by small tablets and overpowering odds. He'd have to leave real resistance to Finn. Drugged or not, his friend wouldn't go down without kicking and screaming. Finn's spirit wouldn't be dulled by inevitability.

Stupidly, Karl couldn't stop himself thinking about Everton Football Club as well. He wondered about the only league that really mattered: finishing above Liverpool at the end of the season. And that made him realise he was going to miss the exquisite pleasure of seeing Liverpool getting knocked out of the European Cup. Yet his feeble smile faded as he wondered if the season and the European Cup would reach a conclusion at all. There might be an end to football and an end to footballers before then.

CHAPTER 9

First, Karl's neck and lips swelled. He felt sick and dizzy as if he'd drunk enough alcohol to take him beyond the pleasantly light-headed stage. His nerves tingled unbearably as if he were on fire from the shoulders upwards. Unseen, a rash ravaged the lining of his throat, partially blocking his airway so that his breathing became audible. It would not be long before his blood pressure plummeted and his organs began to fail.

He had no real idea of time. He knew he'd come to this house on Sunday. It must be Monday. Or was it Tuesday by now? Was it morning, afternoon or night? There was no clue in the chamber and Karl's body clock seemed to have stopped altogether.

Mr Dee's voice rang in his ears. 'As you will have gathered, the time's come to try Anti-MP. Take one tablet now, please.'

Obediently, Karl's fingers fumbled for the bottle. In a daze, he knocked it off the table. He had to go down on his hands and knees to find it and pick it up again. Then he battled with the childproof lid for a minute before he could unscrew it. He swigged back a pill with some of the water, knowing that everything he swallowed was contaminated. It didn't matter any more. The fatal bacteria were multiplying in the caged animals, on surfaces, inside Karl. His lungs, throat, nose and mouth were already teeming with the invisible creatures.

The room spun around him and he flopped onto the chair.

He thought about how this whole thing had begun. On that Saturday, just four weeks ago, if he'd had one more or one less computer game with Finn, they'd have left the block of flats at a different time and missed Dr Perry's accident. Weston Smith and Angus Kerven would have caught up with Dr Perry, stripped her of the lab book and destroyed it. Karl and Finn wouldn't be in this mess, facing death. Right now, they'd be watching telly, hanging out, nicking chocolate from the supermarket, or doing any one of a hundred ordinary, fun things that wouldn't put their lives in danger.

The more Karl thought about it, the more he realised that life revolved around split-second coincidences. If Eve Perry had dashed across the road a fraction of a second earlier or later, she would not have been run over. If Karl and Finn had loitered for a moment longer outside the Brontë Youth and Community Centre before going down Brownlow Hill that Saturday lunchtime, everything would have been different. If they'd called at the shop for chocolate, their whole lives would have changed course. The future of the entire country would have changed. If the driver who'd mown down Dr Perry had stalled his engine at the lights up the road or missed his gear by the bus-stop, or got a puncture or . . . But he didn't. He arrived on the scene at precisely the same time as Eve Perry, exactly when Karl and Finn were strolling past.

It was as if someone had conspired to bring together all of the players at the exact same place in the very same instant. It was as if someone had delayed Weston Smith and Angus Kerven on purpose, as part of the same grand design. Maybe that was why Ruth and Mr Dee believed in God. For them, all these amazing twists of fate couldn't happen purely by chance. They were firm evidence of a God who was orchestrating everything. And that would convince them that they were carrying out His will.

Karl believed more in bad luck than in God.

Inside Karl, the bug shrugged off the only treatment that had stopped it in its tracks before. The cameras in his dungeon recorded a human guinea-pig's uninterrupted deterioration.

Mr Dee must have been delighted.

A second tablet was equally ineffective. Karl felt pus-filled blisters pulling at his nose and mouth, stretching his skin to breaking point and beyond. His throat was so sore that the air he dragged past it felt like sandpaper. His chest seemed to be full of boiling water. Pain racked his muscles and he experienced an overwhelming weakness, far beyond tiredness. With two hard lumps extending downwards from the roof of his mouth like extra teeth and the foul taste of blood on his tongue, he imagined himself as a vampire. He was as good as dead.

PART 5

JUDGEMENT

CHAPTER 1

Mrs Pallister didn't seem to understand her son's predicament. To Grace and Shaughney, she didn't appear to be with it at all. She shrugged at the girls and muttered, 'Always in trouble. Always bother.' She shook her head and then lit another cigarette. 'I suppose the police'll be round again.' Grey-blue smoke surrounded her like a fog.

Grace gave up trying to explain what might have happened. 'Look. Can we borrow Finn's dog? That's all we need right now. Maybe he can . . . Anyway, we just want Bouncer.'

'Help yourselves. His lead's in the kitchen someplace. And if you find Finn, tell him to get his arse in gear. I need him here.'

The Alsatian wasn't used to travelling by Merseyrail and he barked for most of the journey. Still, Grace hoped that he would make up for the embarrassment when they reached West Kirby.

Pointing to the concrete ramp down to beach, Grace said, 'Let's try there. Jo said this is where the FRC hold their stupid services, so maybe Finn . . .' She pulled Bouncer away from a yapping Yorkshire terrier.

Shaughney had tagged along with her friend but she looked fed up because she seemed to think they were on a wild-goose chase.

Trying to get the dog's attention, Grace yanked on his lead. 'Come on, Bouncer. Play the game. Where's Finn?'

The Alsatian pricked up his ears. The mention of his master's name had definitely got through to his canine brain.

Grace squatted down. 'Find Finn,' she muttered. 'That's a good boy. Where's Finn?'

Abruptly, Bouncer was alert. Recently, he'd proved himself to be a total coward, but maybe – just maybe – he could make amends by being a scout. He dragged Grace towards a shop on the road that ran parallel to the marine lake. He spent an age there, sniffing the ground and brickwork, then he looked up at the two girls and let out something between a bark and a whine.

Grace beamed at Shaughney. 'That's it. He's on the scent.'

'Maybe,' Shaughney replied. 'Or he's got the whiff of a bone. Alsatians aren't exactly renowned as sniffer dogs, you know.'

Grace refused to cave in to pessimism. She patted the dog's head and said, 'Good boy. Find him, Bouncer. Find Finn. That's it.'

And off they went. With Bouncer's nose grazing the pavement, they walked back up the lane towards the main road. Guided by Finn's pet, they didn't turn right towards the Merseyrail station, but left towards Hoylake.

Often, the dog stopped, turned back for a while, then picked up the trail again. Sometimes, he seemed certain. Other times, he looked lost and bemused. Half a mile along Meols Drive, they emerged from the town of West Kirby. On their left, there were a few stylish properties lining the edge of the Royal Liverpool Golf Club. On their right was Hoylake Golf Club.

'You can't swing a cat for golf courses round here,' Shaughney noted. 'Crazy.' She hesitated then said, 'I don't mean crazy golf. I mean normal golf's crazy.'

Opposite a very plush estate of about five large properties, Bouncer came to a halt. He'd found the intriguing scent of food, another dog, or Finn. He went right round a bush three times.

'The local dogs probably pee against it,' Shaughney observed.

'Or Finn stopped here.'

'Why would he do that?'

Grace tried to urge Bouncer on. 'Is it Finn?'

Plainly confused, the dog wanted to cross the road towards an ironwork gate that protected the private drive of the classy houses. They waited for a couple of cars to go past and then they charged across. Bouncer dragged them to the left of the gate where there were yet more bushes.

'More dog pee?' Shaughney wondered.

Bouncer looked up and barked.

Grace shook her head. 'No. Finn was here. I'm sure.'

Shaughney was reluctant to agree, but she had to admit that the dog seemed to be on to something. 'Hmm. Maybe.'

When Bouncer began to zigzag towards the gate itself, the girls looked at each other and shrugged. 'It's locked. No chance of getting through,' Grace said. 'There might be a hole in the fence further round. Let's check it out.'

'If you want,' Shaughney replied without much enthusiasm.

They coaxed the dog into the narrow gap between the hedge and the railings surrounding the estate. There was so little space that, in places, they had to go sideways, scraping against the bushes. They hadn't gone far before shrubs blocked their way altogether and Shaughney gave up. 'They didn't come down here. Not a hope.'

Bouncer was equally unconvinced. He had lost the scent and all interest.

Grace came to a stop with a sigh. 'Agreed. Let's try the other side of the gate.'

But it was the same. The estate seemed to be completely caged by tall railings. There was no sign of a way in, except through the main entrance, and no hint of the boys.

'There's nothing doing here,' Shaughney muttered.

'We've got to get Bouncer back on track,' Grace said. 'Let's go over the road again.'

Almost at once, the Alsatian got back into the swing of it. He started to pull Grace further towards Hoylake. Within a few minutes, he amazed the girls by crossing the main road again and turning into a drive that led into the Royal Liverpool Golf Club.

'Blimey!' Shaughney cried. 'Not Karl and Finn.'

But Grace was convinced that Bouncer knew best. 'Where's Finn? That's right. Find him.'

'These places are fussy about who they allow to play,' Shaughney said with a grin. 'Karl and Finn aren't . . .'

Bouncer didn't make for the clubhouse. Nose on the grass, he took off at speed down the side of the fairways. They were going parallel to Meols Drive, back in the direction they'd just come from.

Even Shaughney believed that Bouncer was on the trail of something important now. She had to jog sometimes to keep up with him.

A golfer waved his club at them from one of the greens and shouted, 'Can I help you girls? You seem to be lost.'

Grace reddened, not sure what to do. After all, they were trespassing on private property.

Shaughney wasn't lost for words. And she never reacted well to being patronised. She yelled, 'No, you can't help and, no, we're not lost.'

'I'll have to tell the stewards.'

'Ooh, I'm scared. Our dog's not called Bouncer for nothing, you know. You don't want to see him when he's angry.'

'Walking your dog's not allowed here.'

'Actually,' Shaughney replied, 'he's a guide dog.'

The golfer glanced at Grace and shied away from a confrontation. 'Oh. Right. I'm sorry.'

Towed by Bouncer, the girls left the golfer and his playing partner open-mouthed.

The Alsatian came to a halt just off the sixth fairway. He got particularly excited as he smelt the grass under one tree and dragged Grace around it four times. Then he put his nose onto a patch of grass and let out a whine.

'Is that it?' Shaughney said in surprise. 'Here and no further?'

'Looks like the end of the line.' Grace got down on her knees and pulled Bouncer's head up. 'What have you found?'

On the turf where he'd put his nose, there was something silvery. Grace parted the blades of grass and, picking it up, she let out a gasp.

'What?' Shaughney asked.

Grace held out a door key on her palm.

'So?'

'Remember? Finn was always fiddling with it. Like you fiddle with your earrings. He must've dropped it here.'

'Are you sure it's his?'

Bouncer put his nose into Grace's hand and whined again.

'See? Bouncer's sure. Good enough for me.' She got up, surveyed the terrain and then pointed to the house with an extensive balcony. 'Isn't that the same house that Bouncer sniffed out on the main road?'

Shaughney peered at it. 'I don't know. Yeah, I think so. One of them anyway.'

'Well, remember what it looks like and we'll go back round and check. If it is . . .' Her voice faded away.

'What?'

'I don't know, but I bet Finn's inside.'

This time, Shaughney didn't argue. She shook her head, though, because it seemed so unlikely. The house was not in Karl and Finn's league.

Within ten minutes, the girls were back at the entrance to the estate with a dog that seemed to know its owner was nearby. As the streetlamps came on automatically at dusk, Grace and Shaughney stood to one side so that, if a car turned in, they wouldn't be in the way.

'But . . .' Grace sighed and mumbled, almost to herself, 'What are we going to do about it?'

'Storm the gates?' But Shaughney wasn't being serious. 'That's what the boys would've done – because they're boys.'

'We're not boys.'

'Well spotted. All those biology lessons have paid off, haven't they?'

Grace glanced at her friend. She was about to tell her off for being frivolous when she realised that Shaughney was joking to cover up her unease. 'Well? Any ideas?'

Shaughney got her mobile out of her pocket and wagged it like an admonishing finger. 'This is the sensible thing to do. If you think this is the right house, I'll call Damian. He'll bring the police.' She paused before adding, 'I'll tell them about the key. But I still don't know how a boy like Finn would end up in a place like this.'

CHAPTER 2

Inspector O'Connell parked his unmarked car on the slip-road to the golf course, out of sight of the estate, and perched on the bonnet. Gathered around him in the darkness were Damian Brack, Ed Hawcroft, the two girls and the Alsatian that would have looked like a police dog if he'd had the proper training and inherent discipline. 'So,' he said to Grace and Shaughney, 'what makes you think Finn's in one of those houses? An untrained dog's nose, the odd whine and a house key.'

Grace nodded nervously and held out her only bit of real evidence.

The detective took it and extracted another key from his pocket. 'When Damian mentioned it on the phone, I went round to Finn's house and borrowed his mother's.' He held both keys together and peered at them closely to see if they matched. When he looked up, he was nodding. 'They're identical. It's Finn's all right.'

Grace almost cheered.

'It doesn't mean a lot, but he must have been here-abouts.'

'Bouncer got excited about one of the houses. I'm sure . . .' Grace looked at O'Connell's sceptical face and gave up trying to persuade him.

'Look. You're probably hoping I'll get a load of burly officers and barge in like they do on the telly, but it doesn't work like that. There are legal procedures and safeguards to go through.'

'Sod that,' Damian replied. 'If we're talking biological weapons, there are scientific procedures and safeguards to go through as well, but I know an emergency when I see one. I'm prepared to barge in.'

Shaughney smiled at him and nodded. 'Yeah. That's right.'

O'Connell had to quell their youthful enthusiasm. Pocketing both keys, he replied, 'I'm not saying I can't do anything. I'm going to knock on the door and ask the owner a few questions, but I can't conduct a search or anything. And if they don't invite me in, I can't force them. Not till I've got a warrant. And to get that, I need more evidence than a key left some distance away on a golf course.'

'Take Bouncer,' Grace suggested. 'He'll bark if Finn's there.'

'Or if they're the people who broke into his flat,' Shaughney added.

'No,' O'Connell replied. 'That's a complication too far.'

Ed Hawcroft walked away from the group by a few

216

metres and, speaking quietly, made a mobile phone call.

Grace didn't trust the major. He was a creepy character who listened intently to everyone else but remained silent and aloof as if he were scheming silently. And he always kept one hand in his coat pocket.

An officer dashed up to O'Connell and handed him a plan of the estate, annotated with the number of each property and the names of all of the owners. Turning on the lights of his car and showing the map to Grace and Shaughney, O'Connell asked, 'Which house did Bouncer sniff out?'

The girls looked at the layout from the perspective of the golf course. 'That one,' Grace replied, putting her finger on number five.

O'Connell nodded. 'Miss Ruth Crowe.'

Grace jumped as she realised that Major Hawcroft was standing behind her, peering sneakily over her shoulder. He turned away again and said something else into his mobile.

'Okay,' Inspector O'Connell said. 'Let's get this show on the road.' He looked at Damian and said, 'I guess you want to tag along.'

'Yes,' Damian replied eagerly. 'I might just see something . . .'

'Fine. If Miss Crowe assumes you're my assistant, that's no problem. But don't claim to be a police officer.

That's against the law.' He turned to the military intelligence officer. 'Ed?'

'Yes. I'm coming in. I'm not bound up in red tape like you. I've already lined up some men to play golf tomorrow. The course will be crawling with them, keeping surveillance. More will be workmen. By morning, they'll be doing emergency maintenance on supply pipes in the estate. And my people will be delivering the mail and newspapers to number five tomorrow.'

The detective turned to the girls and said, 'One of my sergeants will stay with you. If you're lucky, she'll treat you to a drink in the clubhouse.'

'Great,' Shaughney replied. 'Mine's a pint of cider.'

As the men got into O'Connell's car, Shaughney nudged Grace. 'Hope we got this right.'

Grace blushed at the thought that they might have made a mistake by misinterpreting Bouncer's reactions.

From the back seat, Damian watched O'Connell lean out of his window and press the button for number five. A terse crackly voice came out of the small speaker. 'Yes?'

'I'm Inspector O'Connell, Merseyside Police, needing to ask you a few questions.'

There was a second of delay. 'Are you sure you've got the right address?' the surprised female voice asked.

'Yes. Miss Ruth Crowe.'

'What are you looking into?'

'I've had a complaint about two boys fooling around and trying to get into the estate – you know, probably making a nuisance of themselves – and I need to check it out.'

'It must be important to send an inspector,' Miss Crowe replied. 'Come on in.'

The gate rolled back darkly to admit the car and then closed behind them. Damian felt as if he'd just been swallowed.

CHAPTER 3

When O'Connell stopped the car by the turning circle and the three of them got out, two bright spotlights glared at them. The detective had barely pushed the door chime when an elderly woman appeared. 'Come in, Inspector O'Connell,' she said softly.

Damian followed him into a spacious hall with curved arches and religious symbols in the alcoves. There was no doubt that this was a wealthy household.

Ruth led the way into the lounge and waved O'Connell towards a luxurious leather armchair. Damian chose to stand. Major Hawcroft walked up and down with his left hand tucked inside his coat pocket.

Damian didn't need to be a police psychologist to interpret Ruth Crowe's expression. She knew by the appearance of three plainclothes men in her house that this was about more than a case of possible antisocial behaviour.

With a wry smile, she sat down and said, 'How can I help you?'

O'Connell seemed intent on keeping up the pretence

for at least a while. 'Have you seen a couple of boys –
teenagers – in or just outside the estate?'

'No.'

'Average height and build. One's got long curly dark
hair, the other's got short light hair, the sort we used to
call a skinhead.'

She lifted her arms from her laps, palms out. 'The
answer's still no.' She paused before adding, 'When
they built this estate, security was uppermost in the
builders' minds. It's a disgrace – very sad – that today's
society forces us to think like that. Anyway, I feel safe
here and I'd certainly know if anyone tried to get in.
Closed-circuit TV, alarms and lights take care of that.'

'Do you live on your own?'

'Yes.'

'Can I take a look at your security measures? I might
be able to suggest improvements . . .'

She rose from her chair serenely. 'This way.'

Off a corridor leading from the hallway, there was a
study that looked like a control room in a supermarket,
intent on catching shoplifters. There were three monitors displaying different black-and-white views: the big
gate, the front of the house, and the back. A sophisticated alarm system was broken down into zones. Each
of them was adorned with a green or orange light. Ruth
pointed to the various zones. 'Windows: all closed.
Doors shut and secure. The downstairs rooms aren't
active because we'd be setting off the alarm right now.

Upstairs: no movement. See? If your tearaways came here, I think I'd know about it, Inspector O'Connell.'

Ruth seemed supremely self-assured. If she was hiding something, she had complete confidence that it would remain hidden. As she glided back to the living room, Damian noted her flowing dress. It was elegant but way out of fashion. Her only items of jewellery were a crucifix and a pale orange band around her wrist. And she didn't dye her hair. It was a mixture of mousy, grey and silver. It suited her.

Back in the lounge, Major Hawcroft took his hand out of his pocket at last. It made him look less shifty and more ready for a fight.

O'Connell examined the image of Christ on a cross, dominating the wall over the mantelpiece. 'You're clearly a religious woman, Miss Crowe.'

'That's not against the law these days, is it?'

The policeman returned her smile. 'I mention it because these boys – they've been known to pick on people who live alone, following them back from church. Which one do you go to?'

'My own.'

'Oh?'

'The Fundamentalist Revolutionary Church.'

Damian got the impression that she expected the police to know about the FRC already and so she did not risk a lie.

Near an ornate table bearing a fancy lamp, Hawcroft

pushed his left hand back into his pocket to resume his normal frosty pose.

'If you don't mind me saying so,' O'Connell replied, 'you don't look like a revolutionary.'

'Not in the sense you mean it, no. But this world – with its out-of-control youngsters like the ones you're after – needs a religious revolution.'

'I gather you're the leader. What does that make you? A priest? Priestess?'

She frowned. 'We don't have formal positions, open to abuse.' She broke eye contact, hesitated and cleared her throat into her hand. 'Just elders.'

'Do you keep a list of your members?'

'How is this relevant?' she asked.

Damian hadn't realised what a smooth operator O'Connell could be. Without any hesitation, he said, 'In case the boys target anyone else in your . . . congregation.'

'It's a church, not a school. I don't have a register.'

Turning the screw a little, O'Connell said, 'Have you heard of a Curtis Bennett?'

'Curtis Bennett. I don't think so.' She appeared to be unruffled.

'Is he – or has he ever been – a member of your church?'

'No.'

'I don't suppose you have much time for modern science,' the detective suggested, changing tack abruptly.

'Why do you say that?'

O'Connell shrugged. 'It doesn't seem to mix with religion. I was thinking about that business with Dr Perry at the university, making life from scratch.'

'I think you've veered away somewhat from intruders and troublesome children,' she replied.

'It's just that I'm struck by your similarity to a description – an e-fit picture – of a woman who attempted to get hold of some information relating to Dr Perry's work.'

'You have me at a disadvantage, Inspector. I thought we were talking about something else entirely.'

The policeman got to his feet. 'Do you mind if we have a quick look around?'

'You've already seen my security.'

'Even so . . .'

She sighed, but agreed. Spreading her arms, she replied, 'Be my guest. Strictly, I think you need a warrant, but I'm not one with anything to hide.'

With the two officers, Damian went from room to room. Each was immaculate, with deep-pile carpeting or polished timber flooring and rugs. He saw nothing that suggested an interest in biology, a clandestine laboratory, or the presence of Finn Pallister and Karl Stephenson.

Damian stopped in the hall to gaze at an imposing reproduction of a painting by Raphael. It was an image of Noah supervising his sons – Ham, Shem and

Japheth – as they built the ark, ready for the great flood.

Coming to a halt beside Damian, Ruth said, 'You don't look like a policeman.'

'No. I'm Damian Brack.'

'So, what are you doing here?'

Damian pointed at the dramatic painting. 'God was displeased with the people He'd created, wasn't He? He decided to drown them all by making it rain for forty days.'

'Not quite everyone. Noah and his wife, and those three sons with their wives went on board. They alone had God's blessing, along with a male and female of every species of animal and insect.'

'Funny,' Damian replied, 'that the ark doesn't look very big.'

'That's artistic licence, Dr Brack.'

'A scientist would put the whole unlikely saga down to artistic licence. If God wanted to destroy humanity, there are far more efficient ways.'

'Are there?'

'Mmm. Like a plague. A Biblical plague. You must have thought about it. What would you do if that happened?'

'That's the difference between us,' she said calmly. 'If the equivalent of Noah's flood happened today, you'd fight against it. I'd accept it and prepare myself, hoping to win God's grace.'

Damian looked into her face and knew for sure that she was the one who intended to set free a biological weapon in God's name. He couldn't prove that a devout and apparently rational woman like Ruth Crowe was a bioterrorist, but he knew. His gut instinct told him and, whilst he had no actual evidence, he'd noticed one slip while he was in her home.

CHAPTER 4

Shaughney and Grace made for the car as soon as it pulled up by the entrance to the golf course. When they joined the cluster of men, Damian was asking O'Connell, 'Do I look old enough to be a doctor?'

The detective frowned. 'Frankly, no. What's that got to do with it?'

'When I told her my name, she seemed to know who I was. She called me Dr Brack. She couldn't have just guessed that I've got a PhD. She must've checked me out and she'd only do that if she had an interest in biology and bacteria.'

O'Connell shook his head. 'First, a dog with an untrained nose. Now a biologist – with a PhD – who thinks he's sniffed out a crime.' He glanced up at the sky as if needing help from above. 'I'll tell you a couple more things. She was similar to Finn's e-fit and there *was* someone else in her house. Maybe a few.'

'How do you know?' said Damian.

'The kitchen. She'd got far too much food for one. There were four mugs drying in the rack as well. And I couldn't see what exactly was parked in the garage, but there was a red sports car. Not her sort of thing. But, if I'm going to pursue a case against her, I need a lot more.'

At last, Hawcroft broke his silence. 'I've got it in hand.'

'Oh?'

For a moment, he took his mobile away from his ear but he left it turned on. 'I put a listening device under the table in her living room and another in the hallway. A couple of my men are monitoring them now.'

The policeman looked shocked. 'That's illegal!'

Ed nodded. 'For you, yes. In matters of national security, I have a little more flexibility.' He nodded towards his mobile and added, 'She hasn't said anything yet. At least not within range.'

Shaughney decided to break into the ring of men. Sidling up to Damian, she said, 'Grace and Bouncer reckon she's hiding Finn and you think she's got a lab somewhere inside. Right?'

'Right.'

'But you didn't see either.'

'No.'

'Doesn't that mean she's got a secret room in the attic or basement or something?' Shaughney raised her eyebrows significantly as she gazed at him.

'Yes. So what?'

'The thing is, no one can keep everything secret.'

'How do you mean?'

If it hadn't been Damian who was being slow on the

uptake, she would have got shirty. 'Well, it's obvious how you could get evidence. Someone must have built it for her. She must have bought all sorts of bits and pieces. Don't you know the people who supply scientific stuff? Can't you check with them?'

Damian nodded and grinned widely. 'Of course! Fantastic idea. In particular, she'd need experimental animals. Thanks to animal rights activists, there aren't many suppliers left.' He got out his phone. 'Thanks, Shaughney.'

'Not just a pretty face.' In the gloom, she peered at her watch. 'But it's late. You won't get anyone now.'

It wasn't until mid-morning on Tuesday that Inspector O'Connell had enough information to act. That was when Damian could confirm that some specialised biological equipment and research animals had been delivered to Ruth's address. It was also then that Hawcroft captured a brief conversation between Ruth and an unknown man about a first human host.

The detective brought his team together in Hoylake police station to develop a plan of action. Rosalind Monkhouse was present only as a ghostly voice. In common with Damian, though, she insisted that speed was the most important thing. The longer that it took to raid the house, the more likely it was that Ruth Crowe's cult would have the weapon ready for use – or already deployed.

O'Connell glanced at the corkboard where a plan of Ruth Crowe's house, provided by the builders, was pinned alongside the aerial view of the estate. 'If we go in and she releases this germ, is there any way of containing it? Can we quarantine the house somehow?' he asked.

Rosalind and Damian both answered firmly at the same time. 'No.'

Apparently addressing the empty air, but actually talking to Professor Monkhouse, the detective said, 'How's *your* work going? Any sign of a cure?'

Rosalind did not sound optimistic. 'It wouldn't be wise to rely on me. I'm trying to stop an antibiotic-resistant infection in full flow. That's near impossible. Damian, what's the obvious angle any scientist would pursue?'

'Dream up a new way of killing it,' he answered without a moment's thought.

'Exactly. That's the natural, understandable reaction. But it hasn't borne much fruit with resistant bacteria recently. That's why MRSA stays one step ahead of us. I've got to throw off this macho idea of slaughtering it. That's a man's way, isn't it? If a little gun can't stop something, wheel out a bigger gun. But if it can't be killed, it can't be killed. End of the road.'

'What else is there?' Damian asked.

'I'm working on it,' Rosalind's voice replied. 'But I'm going to have to be cleverer than attack, attack, attack.

It won't be easy. Or quick. I'm trying to "talk" to it instead of declaring war.'

'What?' O'Connell exclaimed. He glanced at Damian, but Rosalind's assistant could only shrug.

'You haven't got the time to listen to my plan,' she replied. 'You do your job and I'll do mine. If you're successful, you won't need me anyway. I won't have to worry about it any more.'

'Okay,' Inspector O'Connell said, banging a fist on the table. 'Let's get this show back on the road. We're going to assume the worst. Inside Ruth Crowe's house, there's a biological weapon and if it gets out, it could wipe out thousands . . .'

'It's not a case of *could* wipe them out,' Damian muttered. 'It *will*.'

'Yeah. So, what do we have to do to keep it safe? Biological procedures take precedence over legal procedure in this operation. So, fill us in, Damian.'

There was silence as they all listened to the young biologist attentively, knowing that their lives – and the lives of their friends and families – depended on getting it right. Major Hawcroft was considering Damian's every word, but he was also thinking his own unfathomable private thoughts.

Facing them all, Damian shivered. He never wanted to be a leader. He wanted an anonymous life, working away behind the scenes on the world's worst bacteria and viruses. But here he was, standing in front of a group of combatants. 'First,' he said, 'you've got to take this on board. It must be stored safely right now because we're not falling down like flies. We've got to keep it that way because Rosalind doesn't want us to rely on her to cure it. That's the number one priority. You see, we can always kill it with bleach or concentrated acid if it's in a dish within a sealed room. But if it gets out – once it's an infection in you or me – we can't hit it with lethal chemicals. They'd kill the human host. But even that'd be after we've spread it around. Once the genie's out of the bottle, we can't put it back in.'

Damian paused for the effect of his words to sink in. 'If you think about it, it means something else as well. You can't go into the house with stun grenades or whatever they're called. In fact, no shooting of any kind. You can't use anything that might damage the fabric of the house because physical damage is what'll let the bacteria out.'

One of the policemen asked, 'What about an incendiary bomb? Wouldn't that burn everything, including this germ?'

Damian shook his head. 'Even if it destroyed ninety-nine point nine per cent, that's not good enough. The rest will be blown around the area and start to multiply. It's got to be one hundred per cent.'

O'Connell cut in. 'But we've got to hit the occupants hard and quick. Before *they've* got a chance to free it.'

Damian shrugged. 'I'm not the police, intelligence or a soldier. I'm just a biologist, telling you what you can't do.' He turned to the plan of house. 'Look. There's no chance of putting a lab in a loft like this. Not enough space, and getting equipment up there isn't going to happen. This is where it'll be.' He tapped the diagram. 'The basement. I'll guarantee that's where the weapon is – and the two boys, I guess. It'll be okay to force your way into the basement but, somewhere inside, there'll be a sealed unit. That's what you don't touch.' With a nervous tingle in his spine, he added, 'That's my job afterwards.'

O'Connell joined him at the front of the team. He peered closely at the layout of the house. 'Unless Crowe's changed things around, there's access to the basement from the utility room here.' Glancing at Ed Hawcroft and Damian, he asked, 'Did either of you get a look inside it last night?'

'No,' Damian answered.

Hawcroft shook his head while still listening to someone on his mobile. 'If speed's the essence, let's get down to the nitty-gritty. I've got one team in place, posing as workmen, digging up supply lines in the estate. I'm in constant contact. They've isolated the electricity cable that goes to the entrance gate. They can take control of it any time. At my say-so, they'll puncture a gas main. The smell will be awful. Someone'll report it. My best units are standing by in

British Gas and Transco vans, ready to go in.'

The detective interrupted. 'I don't recall an order to hand this operation over to military intelligence.'

'Just helping out,' Hawcroft replied. 'But let's not argue over rank. My troops are specially trained for this sort of situation. The best. They'll make sure Ruth Crowe's boiler breaks down. According to British Gas, her boiler's in her utility room. Perfect. My men will call to fix it.'

O'Connell considered it for a few seconds. 'She'll be mighty suspicious.'

'Yes. But they're professionals. Very convincing. Once one's in – and taken Crowe out of the equation – the men outside will cut power to her security cameras. Have you got a better idea?'

O'Connell faced the team. 'Anyone?'

There was silence.

'All right,' Ed Hawcroft said. 'According to my people – playing golf and delivering mail – everything's quiet right now. And there's no panic or activity according to the microphones.'

Someone else asked, 'Shouldn't we evacuate the other houses?'

O'Connell shook his head. 'That'd make it too obvious we're making a move.'

Damian added, 'And it won't save any lives if we mess it up.'

Major Hawcroft was itching to put his training to

good use. 'I'm giving the order to sabotage the gas supply. All right?'

'Just make sure they don't blow the house up,' Damian replied. 'That'd be the quickest way to scatter the weapon over the whole of Merseyside. In days, you'll have the not-yet-dead burning the dead in the streets.'

CHAPTER 5

The heavy gate drew slowly back and two industrial vans rolled into the estate. At once, a couple of men in fluorescent yellow jackets jumped out and closed off a rectangle of land in yellow and black warning tape. At the gate and on the drive, they propped up two signs bearing a warning triangle, an image of an explosion, and the words *No smoking, no naked flames*. One of the brawny engineers shouted to the workmen, 'Hey! Who's been careless with the pickaxe again?' He looked into the hole they'd dug, shook his head and laughed. 'Are you on some crazy job creation scheme? If you are, thanks.' Talking to his own unit, he said, 'Okay, let's close this whole section down.' He glanced at the schematic in his hands. 'Here you go. The valve's over there. Ben, knock on every door and tell them what's going on, will you?'

In the mobile headquarters parked in the lane to the golf course, a deep voice from the speaker said quietly, 'Green Leader to Chief. Stage one complete. On my way to number five.'

Major Hawcroft seemed tense but cheerful. To the others in the van, he said, 'It's started. His name's Ben. Top dog in my top squad.'

Carrying a clipboard and wired with a hidden microphone, Ben strode confidently up to the front door in his British Gas overalls. His colleagues hadn't disabled the house's security system because that would have been too suspicious. The Chief's judgement was that a simultaneous gas leak and power cut were too much to swallow. Ben banged on the door, rang the bell twice and then took a step back.

He was in operations mode, alert, ready for combat. He knew exactly what he had to do, his training was impeccable, and he had a brilliant team behind him.

He recognised the woman who opened the door. He'd studied her e-fit but, in the role of gas engineer, he showed no sign of knowing her. Ben glanced down at his clipboard. 'Er . . . Mrs Crowe?'

'Miss.'

'Right, love. Your gas is going off. Sorry, but you can't have missed the smell.' He held out his identification. 'Best if you turn your boiler off. That way, it'll come back on easier when we're done. Are you happy with that, or do you want me to do it? Two minutes and I'm out of your hair.'

She peered across at the yellow-jacketed workmen and the warning triangle. 'Well . . .'

'If you like, I'll come back after and turn it on again. Check everything's hunky-dory. All part of the service.'

'Okay.' She stood to one side.

Ben stepped into the hallway, and out of shot of the security camera. Instantly, he reverted to his role of elite soldier. He dropped the clipboard and produced a wet rag from behind it. In less than a second, he had Ruth Crowe in an armlock and the cloth clamped over her nose and mouth. In his powerful arms, she took three breaths of the vapour and then went limp.

Ruth's closed-circuit television went dead and five fake technicians ran up the path and joined Ben inside. Three would follow Ben. The other two would go from room to room, securing the property and dealing with any resistance.

'Blue Leader to Chief. Stage two complete. Green Team inside. Intruder alarm system down. All quiet outside.'

Proud of his men, Hawcroft boasted, 'Won't be long. Clockwork so far.'

Ben went first. Down the corridor and into the utility room. For a moment, he couldn't see the join in the vinyl flooring. It was beautifully disguised. He bent down and rolled back the patterned plastic. Above him, two sturdy comrades kept watch.

Slowly, Ben lifted up the trapdoor to reveal wide

wooden steps down into the basement, dimly lit by a lamp in the wall. At the bottom, there was a conventional door.

For big men, they could move surprisingly stealthily. Neither Ben nor the three specialists behind him made a sound as they descended the stairs.

Ben checked the structure of the door and decided to crash straight through it. That was his best chance of taking its occupants by surprise. Opening it would give anyone inside an extra split second to react. He would have preferred to barge in with armed colleagues covering him, but he was alone in carrying a firearm and that was to be used only as a last resort.

Hawcroft turned up the volume and concentrated. The voice in the loudspeaker was barely audible, but the message was clear and simple. 'Green Team going in. Stage three.'

Ben's shoulder was stronger than the door. When he slammed into it, the wood around the catch splintered and his momentum propelled him into the basement. Two of his colleagues followed him inside and the third took up a position at the broken doorway.

Ben came to an instant judgement about the four people in the room. A boy tied to a chair was a hostage. He was not a threat, but he might need protection. The man who staggered back against a bench was too shocked to pose an immediate risk; he was not a combatant. The two men by the door considered themselves hard; they were a potential menace and needed to be neutralised first. Both pulled out knives.

The bigger of the two advanced on Ben. But he was an amateur. When his partner was poleaxed from behind by one of Ben's team, the fool glanced over his shoulder at the noise. Ben didn't need any other prompt. A swift kick broke the man's wrist and sent the knife flying across the laboratory. A punch made him double up. Within seconds, he was a harmless bundle on the floor with his arms tied behind his back.

When Ben spun round, he swore under his breath. The third man had picked up the knife from where it lay by the chemical protection suit and was holding it to the boy's throat. His other hand hovered over a keypad.

Ben's eyes were fixed on the final opponent, but he spoke to the lad in the chair. 'Are you Karl? Or is it Finn?'

'Finn,' the boy strained to reply. 'Karl's—'

'You'll talk to *me*,' the man said, interrupting.

'Fine. What's your name? Just to make it easier.'

The man hesitated before answering, 'James.'

Ben nodded. 'Is it Jim or do you prefer James?' he asked to make sure that Major Hawcroft had heard.

'James.'

'That's good. And I'm Ben.' He decided not to push

for a surname yet. Instead, he looked around the room and said, 'Fancy set-up you've got down here. I guess that makes you a scientist. But we've taken over the rest of the house. You're trapped.'

James shrugged. 'Doesn't bother me. You must've been told what I've been working on. Judgement and death don't frighten me.'

'True,' Ben answered. He hadn't whipped out his gun because there was a door with a biohazard warning behind James. The integrity of that chamber was Ben's only imperative. If a bullet hit and penetrated it, hell would be let loose. Of course, this James would call it the opposite of hell.

There were two monitors at the far end of the laboratory. Ben couldn't make out details from where he stood, but he thought that they both showed a second boy slumped on the floor of a small room. It was probably Karl Stephenson. If so, he was beyond help.

'Let Finn go,' Ben said calmly. 'There's no point hurting him.'

James smiled insanely. 'You don't really care about him – or me. You're interested in the germ, that's all.'

He was right. To Ben, everyone in the basement was expendable, including himself. He'd mentioned Pallister only to help the Chief build up an image of what was happening. Ed Hawcroft's voice in his earpiece reassured him, 'I'm hearing it all.'

'The instrument of retribution is ready and it scares

241

you! You can't run from it.' James moved his left hand and said, 'All I have to do is hit this button and the door's released. It doesn't matter what you do to me.'

Outside in the van, Damian frowned. 'That's not right. It doesn't work like that.'

'How do you mean?' Hawcroft snapped.

'There's got to be two doors with a sort of airlock in between. It's where soiled air can be sucked out, protective clothing bleached and contamination scrubbed off,' Damian explained as quickly as he could. 'For safety, you can only open the second door manually from inside the airlock.'

'Sure?' O'Connell checked.

'Yes.'

'Could he have rigged it to open both doors at the same time? Remember, he always was going to let it out at some point.'

Damian hesitated.

'I need an answer,' Hawcroft urged. 'Ben needs an answer.'

'They're just not built like that,' Damian replied. 'No, I don't think so.'

Hawcroft turned on his microphone. 'Chief to Green Leader. He's bluffing. There's an inner door. Take him down before he gets through the first one.'

CHAPTER 6

In shock, Finn watched the unfolding events. The nearest policeman or soldier – or whatever he was – had a warped smile on his face. 'Yes, I'm scared – about what you're prepared to do to kids like Finn. But me and my men aren't scared of dying. It comes with the job. Soldiers and religious fundamentalists lumped together, eh?'

Finn's head was fit to burst. James Dee and these mad church people had chained him to a chair for ages, threatened him, drugged him, done unmentionable things to his best mate. Now, the people who'd come to rescue him were hinting that he was scared. Scared? Never. Not enough to admit it, anyway. He was far more angry than scared.

He shook his head from side to side, trying to clear his brain of the deadening effects of the tablets. He looked down at his ankle and judged the length of loose chain attached to the floor. Then he waited. The knife in Mr Dee's hand wavered. Sometimes it was near his throat, sometimes it drifted up closer to his nose. Sometimes, as the teacher concentrated on the soldier, it was several centimetres away. A decent gap was all that Finn needed. He planted both feet firmly on the floor and tensed, ready to spring as far as the chain would allow.

'Back off,' Mr Dee said, staring at the big bloke in a gas man's uniform. 'Or I'll open the door.'

'I don't think so,' Ben replied. 'You're ready to die. If you could release this weapon right now, you'd have done it already. What are you waiting for?'

Mr Dee was looking at the soldier a bit like he eyeballed a badly-behaved pupil. He didn't like defiance. 'Back off!' he cried again, not paying attention any more to his second human guinea-pig.

Finn launched himself sideways, chair and all, into Mr Dee's legs and the teacher let out a yowl.

Out of the corner of his eye, Finn saw the gas man flying through the air. One of his powerful legs whistled past Finn's ear and the man's shoe thudded into Mr Dee's chest. There was a sickening crunch and a charge by at least two other men. It was all reduced to a blur.

The only thing that Finn took in was a voice. 'Green Leader to Chief. Situation under control. Four opposition casualties. One boy assumed dead. One rescued, ready for evacuation. Request science backup. Biohazard door clicked open. Inner door presumed sealed.'

*

For security, three of Major Hawcroft's special forces were still stationed in the basement, as if they were protecting the crown jewels. Of course, the secret laboratory held something far more valuable and dangerous than gold and diamonds.

Shock drained the blood from Damian's face. His stomach churned as he stood in front of the two monitors, hardly able to believe the grotesque scene inside the sealed crypt. A lifeless curled body was all that remained of the bright and brave boy who'd provided the Anti-MP cure. Karl deserved a medal, not this. Turning aside, Damian put his hands over his mouth and swallowed, trying not to vomit.

Ed asked him, 'Are you all right?'

Damian shook his head. 'No. Are you? You're not human if you can look at this and . . .'

'According to you, we could've had a death toll of thousands, but we lost one boy,' the major replied. 'It's not nice to see, but we won. One fatality is a let-off. It's an absolute triumph.'

'That's all right, then,' Damian snapped with sarcasm. 'Just a clean-up to do and we can all have a party.'

Unlike the members of his elite units, the major hesitated for a second.

In that instant, Damian saw straight through him. 'No, no, no! Decontamination and that's all. There's nothing else to do here. Don't even think about keeping a sample.'

245

'In the interests of the future defence of this country . . .'

'No!'

'We need to work out a way of beating a weapon like
this. If we're going to do that, we need a sample . . .'

'There's no way of doing it safely. No way at all. It's
going to take me long enough just to work out how to
clear this mess up.'

Damian remembered his last tantrum. He'd had a
handful of his mother's blanket at the time and he'd
thumped his father as hard as he could. As a five-year-
old, he hadn't been able to wake up his mum. Right
now, he felt the same hopelessness because he could
not bring back Karl Stephenson either.

He peered through the tiny gap into the airlock. 'It
looks okay for now but I can't say for sure, not till I'm
in full gear. I'll tell you one thing,' he continued
angrily, 'Mrs Stephenson won't have a body to bury
when I've finished. Why don't you go and tell her
that, while I figure out how to bleach everything, dis-
solve what's left in acid, before I get the whole
basement encased in concrete forever? Including
Karl's remains. Maybe that'll take the edge off your
absolute triumph.'

'I've got my orders and you know what they say
about soldiers and their orders. They're given to us by
Government and we obey them without question.'

'Professor Monkhouse is the world leading authority

on bacterial infections and she hasn't managed to beat it. What makes you think . . .?'

'I don't think, Damian. I just . . .'

'Yeah. I know. Follow orders. But your orders are crazy. Suicide. Whoever's giving them needs to see this bloodbath. Let them come and see Karl. Then maybe . . .' Damian stopped yelling and said, 'Hang on.'

'What is it?'

He looked around the laboratory, especially the desk. Frantically, he asked, 'Where's Eve Perry's lab book?'

Hawcroft shrugged. 'We've already looked for it. No joy yet.'

Damian rounded on the major. 'Have you taken it?'

'No.'

That book had become the Fundamentalist Revolutionary Church's bible. Whoever had it could start the whole project again. Accusing the military policeman, Damian said, 'You've got it, haven't you?'

'Think about it. If I had the instruction book, I wouldn't have to keep a sample of the biological weapon, would I?'

It was a good point. Damian calmed down a little. 'All right. But we've *got* to find it.'

'O'Connell's people are searching the premises. It'll be here somewhere. Maybe it's in there with Karl Stephenson.' He nodded towards the door with the red warning.

'Unlikely.' Damian sighed.

'All right. Let's call a truce,' Ed replied. 'While this search is going on, I'll talk to a certain Government department. I'll explain what's happening and tell them your professional judgement. We'll put everything on hold till I get a response. Okay?'

Damian hesitated and then agreed. 'I suppose so. Right now, I've got plenty of other things to worry about. I want to study the way water's delivered to the chamber and how air gets pumped in and out. And how contaminated equipment gets dealt with. I've got to work out how to use the same system to flood the place with lethal chemicals.' He sat down at the control panel and concentrated on the daunting task.

Half an hour later, he announced, 'I've got some ideas. But before I do anything, I'm going out to the van to consult Rosalind.'

Hawcroft nodded. 'Fair enough. We'll hold the fort.'

But as soon as Damian began to climb the stairs, the major signalled to one of his men and pointed to the protective suit. 'This is it. You know what you've got to do. In you go, and make it quick.'

CHAPTER 7

Finn didn't trust anyone in authority. Not the police, not those special troops, certainly not church leaders, and not teachers. None of them. He might've trusted Damian Brack or Rosalind Monkhouse but he wasn't convinced that they could pull rank on the others. If he'd left the lab notebook in that awful place, he was sure it'd end up with someone who'd screw things up again. His brain may have been addled by everything that had happened but he knew what he had to do. When everyone else was fussing about in the basement, he'd slipped the book inside his clothing.

The only person Finn trusted without question was gone. Nothing would ever be the same again. No more Everton matches, no more secret cider down by the docks, no more messing about at school or bunking off, no more Teen and Toddler Scheme, no more computer games. No more Karl and no more fun.

Finn sat on the cold ground next to Bouncer and warmed himself by the bonfire that he'd created out of sticks and rubbish. He no longer had his friend to help him decide what to do, but he knew what was the right thing tonight. 'Here goes,' he said. Despite the heat of the fire, he shivered as he grasped the thick blue laboratory book and flicked through its indecipherable pages for the last time. Then he muttered, 'This is for Karl.'

He tossed the book to the hungry flames and, just to make sure, he prodded it with a stick until it was well alight. Then he propped himself up on his arms and watched the private cremation.

The flickering light reflected from Shaughney's earrings and made the hoops twinkle. Her voice trembled as she said, 'You know, for a fifteen-year-old boy, Karl wasn't bad.'

Without lifting his eyes from the fire, Finn replied, 'He was more than that. And he was clever. Cleverer than me. But he still went first.'

Grace sniffed. 'We should've saved him.' Then she started sobbing once more. 'We messed it up.'

'I know what you mean,' Shaughney said quietly to her friend, 'but we didn't mess up. Not really. Maybe it doesn't feel like it right now, but we did all right.'

'Did we?'

'It was us – and Bouncer – who found the cult's house. We guided the police. Without us, no rescue.' Her eyes moist, she gazed at Grace and added, 'No Finn.'

'I don't know how you can be so pleased . . .'

Shaughney put an arm around her friend's shoulders. 'I'm not. I'm just as choked as . . . But someone's got to remind us we did all we could and Karl didn't die for nothing. If we hadn't found this biological warfare thing, everyone would be dead. Everyone! It was us young 'uns who showed them the way.'

Grace shrugged. 'I suppose.'

'I just hope they don't mess it up now they haven't got us helping any more,' Shaughney replied, 'but they probably will, because they're adults.'

Grace watched the flames dancing on the remains of Eve Perry's laboratory notes. 'Don't forget Finn. He did the most important thing. He grabbed the notebook. At least they can't use that again.' She turned towards him and said, 'You were brave, the way you clobbered that stupid teacher.'

'Doesn't bring Karl back,' Finn mumbled.

'I wish God . . .' Grace's voice trailed away into the night.

'What?' Shaughney asked.

'Nothing.'

Shaughney smiled wryly. 'If you're thinking of resurrection, He doesn't work like that. Even though Karl didn't deserve what he got.'

'I know. God gives people freedom, a chance, they blow it, and that's that. The innocent suffer.' Grace shook her head ruefully.

Finn didn't really follow what they were talking about. His mind had drifted elsewhere. He watched the burning book in silence until there was nothing left but ash.

CHAPTER 8

Miles away, in her own experimental chamber, Rosalind lifted both arms. Her fists reached for the ceiling and she cried, 'Brilliant! Great job, Damian. You know I always had faith in you.' She laid her hands on her stomach. 'And Junior says thanks as well. You've given him or her an amazing present: a world to live in.'

In one respect Rosalind was like Ed Hawcroft. Much as she loathed the loss of even one life, especially that of a young person, she regarded the operation as a huge success. A mere one death was beyond her wildest expectations.

Knowing that Damian still had a dreadful job to do, she settled down again. She listened as Damian talked through the options for destroying every last residue of the nightmare and added some thoughts of her own. Then they agreed on the safest possible method.

Damian was about to sign off, when he turned away from the camera. 'Hang on.'

Rosalind frowned. 'What's wrong?'

'I don't know. There's something going on outside.

Just a . . .' Distracted, he said, 'Someone's shouting for me.'

He went out of shot for three minutes. It wasn't long, but the wait seemed endless. It was ample time for Rosalind's heart – and all her hopes – to sink. She was wrong to think that such elation could last. Some instinct told her that the outcome was just too good. A sudden anxiety churned her stomach, her entire body tingled, nausea swept over her, and her breath came in short shallow gasps.

When Damian reappeared on her screen, his face was white. To all intents and purposes, he was a ghost. He could hardly speak. 'I've got to go, Rosalind. Not that it'll do any good. It's that stupid fool, Hawcroft . . .'

'He hasn't . . .' But she knew he had. He'd sent someone into the sealed chamber to collect a sample of the biological weapon and something had gone wrong. 'What's happened?'

'One of Hawcroft's team was a military chemist. He went in to get a petri dish. After, when he took the gear off, they saw a wet patch on his clothes.' Damian paused and looked away from the camera. He was too shocked to be logical and coherent. 'It was when they rescued Finn. There was some sort of struggle with a knife. It shot across the room and must have gashed the protective suit. No one noticed. In a hurry, this chap didn't do the standard checks.'

'So, he's breathed it and his clothing's contaminated.

He's brought it out into the world.'

Damian nodded. With heavy sarcasm, he muttered, 'All for the defence of his country.'

Rosalind didn't need video-conferencing. As she spoke to Damian by phone twenty-four hours after exposure, her imagination filled in an appalling picture. Actually, she didn't need much imagination either. She'd turned off the sound on her TV while Damian was on the line, but all channels were broadcasting continuous news. Every programme beamed images of panic, police, swarming people, and soldiers into her silent laboratory. Soon, the medical services and undertakers would be overrun.

'I never did ask you, Damian. I guess we were always too busy working. But have you got anyone . . . you know . . . close to you?'

'A girlfriend, you mean? No.' For a moment, he went quiet. Then he added, 'Just as well, the way things have turned out. But . . .'

'What?'

'You must have. What about your partner?' His voice was like gravel, weary and defeated.

Rosalind steeled herself. 'When society's about to go into meltdown, you need doctors, nurses, the police and so on. He's a lawyer.' She sniffed, holding back her emotion. 'What use is a lawyer? Who's he going to take to court?'

'He's more than that,' Damian replied. 'He's Junior's father. We need people who love us as well.'

Rosalind cried, 'Hey. Don't do this to me. I'm supposed to be consoling you.'

'Shall I tell you something that'll help?'

'I could use that.'

'The Government's got a shelter to protect themselves against a nuclear blast, but not this. They're in the firing line as well.'

'It's not all bad news, then.' Rosalind's chuckle was forced and pathetic.

'You said you were talking to the bacterium rather than waging war on it,' Damian said. 'Does that mean you've got a new line of research?'

'I'm getting there.'

Damian nodded. 'I always had faith in you as well. You'll crack it.'

Rosalind wasn't as confident as Damian that she'd succeed. But she wasn't going to admit it to him. 'Not quick enough, but I'm going to make it useless for germ warfare.'

'Great.' He let out a frightful cough. 'Tell me what you're doing. I want to think about how this horrible organism's going to meet its end.'

She would allow him his wish. If he wanted to imagine his revenge on the bacterium while he bowed out, she wouldn't disillusion him with her doubts. 'No problem,' she said.

CHAPTER 9

Sealed within her bubble, Rosalind wasn't simply weary. Her whole demeanour on the video sequence betrayed her exhaustion, as if she been drained of all the physical and mental strength that she once had in abundance. There was nothing left but grim determination to finish something that she'd started. When she wiped her nose with the back of her hand, the bracelets on her scraggy wrist seemed very loose. Her face was blotchy and lined as if she'd aged ten years.

She inhaled deeply, shuffled in her seat and looked up towards the ceiling before trying to present a businesslike image. 'How do you stop resistant bacteria? That's what I asked a few days ago. How long ago? I'm not sure. Anyway, bacteria are like school bullies. They only turn nasty if they're convinced they've got the strength and numbers to overwhelm their victim. If they don't, they back off. They don't become virulent. They're cowards really.'

She took a breather to gather her own strength. 'Think about it. They only attack if they've amassed enough numbers to swamp the host's immune system, so they must be able to estimate their own numbers. How do they do that? I checked. They send out a chemical signal to each other. They all detect this signal and gauge its concentration. The more of them there are, the greater the concentration. It's almost as good as counting. It's called quorum-sensing because the bacteria only infect a living creature when there's lots of them, like a committee that only takes decisions when it's got a quorum.' She smiled feebly. 'Nice comparison. It's a clever trick – and a weak point.'

Her eyes drifted away from the camera before she attempted the role of lecturer again. 'So, this bug doesn't turn its virulence gene on if it can't mount a successful infection. Keep it turned off permanently and you've got a way to stop it. That's what I've done. I've made a chemical that'll block the bacterium's line of communication. I'm calling it QSB for quorum-sensing blocker. It doesn't kill them, but they can't give off their signal when QSB's around. That means every single bacterium can't sense its mates. They all think they're alone and they don't attempt to infect anything. It lulls them into a false sense of weakness.' She spread her tired arms. 'There you are. The best I can do. I've made peace with the bacteria rather than kill them. And it works in here with lab mice. But what about people?' She shrugged. 'Human hosts should stay well if they're dosed with QSB because the bacteria won't attack. All being well, a decent immune system should then pick them off one by one.'

She pointed at the television screen in the corner of her confines. 'I hear on the news that it's spreading. Reporters are obsessed with numbers as well, aren't they? Hundreds infected. Thousands. I don't know.' She shook her head sadly.

'It won't stop, you know. It'll be a pandemic unless . . .' She sighed.

'I haven't finished my tests. I can't without sick people to work on. So, what do I do? I've made this film and emailed my results to every overseas specialist I can think of. If the next step goes wrong, they can see what I've done, learn from it, and try again. But Damian had faith in me. I'm putting my faith in QSB. I've protected myself with it and I'm coming out. That makes me and Junior the first human guinea-pigs. It's going to be strange, leaving this place. Cramped, horrid, but safe. Anyway, I'll see for myself what sort of world my child is going to inherit. That's if QSB works and we survive.' She hesitated and then added, 'You know, it's a nifty idea. It's got a chance. Enough for me to risk my life – and Junior's life – on it.' She tried to look upbeat as she signed off. 'That's it. End of programme. No rest for the wicked. There's a lot of people out there who need my help.'

Rosalind leaned forward awkwardly and turned off the camera.

After the public screening of the harrowing video sequence, there was a moment of silence. Then came loud applause. The chairman allowed the audience its say. He let the clapping and cheering go on for a minute, two minutes, three minutes. Then he stood up and approached the microphone with the medal in his hand.

'I've had the pleasure of giving out a few of these,' he

announced. 'Each time, I've said something about the recipient making a significant advance in biology, somehow changing the world in which we live for the better. But I've never before given it to someone who has saved literally thousands, possibly millions of lives.' He turned his head and held out an arm. 'Professor Rosalind Monkhouse.'

A heavily pregnant Rosalind climbed up onto the stage as the ovation began all over again.

In the audience, Shaughney was wearing a slight inexplicable smile. Grace nudged her friend and whispered, 'What are you grinning about?'

'I was thinking about Karl. Round at my house, when he saw Professor Monkhouse's bump, he thought she was just getting fat. He was so embarrassed!'

Grace made a tutting noise with her tongue. 'This isn't the time and place for—'

Finn interrupted her. 'No. She's right. That's the sort of thing I want to remember. The fun bits. That's what Karl would . . .'

On the platform, Rosalind shook the chairman's hand, took the medal and leaned towards the microphone. At once, the spectators quietened to silence and settled back into their seats. On such an occasion, they expected a long speech.

'It's . . . er . . . It's with regret that I accept this honour,' Rosalind said hesitantly. 'You see, when I lie awake at night, I can't think of those thousands. I can only think of all those I didn't work quickly enough to help.' She paused and glanced at the three young people in the room before adding, 'This is for Karl Stephenson and Damian Brack.' Then she turned and hurried from the stage.

HURRICANE FORCE BY MALCOLM ROSE

What would happen if we could use the weather as a weapon?

Jake's father died in mysterious circumstances – now Jake, who shares a similar skill for predicting the weather, takes on his mantle. But can he prevent his father's research falling into the wrong hands, and stop the US military from using it for nefarious means?

Award-winning author and research scientist, Malcolm Rose, turns his formidable talent to warfare, and the weather.

ISBN: 0-689-87284-4